THE DYNAMITE YANKEE

The Cuban rebels called him Captain Ratonero — the rat-catcher. But the rats that were caught in his dynamite traps were a lot more deadly than common rodents. For they were the hated, murderous troops of a foreign tyranny.

But Captain Ratonero was no Cuban. He was a young American engineer fresh from New England, and he owed his peculiar new role in a guerrilla war not of his own choice to three powerful arguments: the cannons of a coast-guard ship, the muzzles of a firing squad, and the arms of a lovely senorita.

DONALD BARR CHIDSEY has made an enviable name for himself both as a writer of excellent historical novels, including such as *This Bright Sword, Captain Crossbones,* and *The Pipes are Calling,* and also as a writer of historical biographies, including those of Sir Walter Raleigh, Marlborough, and Bonnie Prince Charlie.

His own life has been as full of adventure as his writings. He has covered a good part of the earth in tramp steamers, pearl shell boats, and private yachts. He has lived in the South Seas, has been a newspaperman, actor, farmer, road gang foreman, mountaineer, boxer and fencer. During the war he served with the British, New Zealanders, Highlanders, the Free French, and the United States Army.

At the present time he lives quietly in Lyme, Connecticut, and seems content to confine further adventures to the pen.

The Flaming Island

by

DONALD BARR CHIDSEY

ACE BOOKS, INC.

23 West 47th Street, New York 36, N. Y.

Other Ace Books by
Donald Barr Chidsey:
THIS BRIGHT SWORD (D-278)
CAPTAIN CROSSBONES (D-318)
THE PIPES ARE CALLING (D-364)

CHAPTER ONE

The sky was opalescent; only a few stars twitched there. The surface of the sea was smeared with dawn. The coast guard boat could be seen plainly now, and so could the shore of Cuba, all humpety-hump with hills, a blue-black horizon. The coast guard boat was low, lean. Spray misted her in a bridal veil, thrown from the waves she made. At the bow, an upthrust nose, was a brass four-pounder. Yet only a little smoke tumbled from her stack, to be whipped off, scattered over the Caribbean.

In contrast, the tug *Hina* spewed smoke in great bulbous black masses. She had been moving at half speed, lest sparks or the glow from the fires show at the stack. When the first rays of the sun discovered the customs cutter, she had been made to dart ahead like a whippet. She strained in every beam, creaking, swaying, as though she wished to fly. On the *Hina* they were burning not only coal, but also — to get up even more pressure — barrel-loads of pine chunks steeped in lard.

"Any chance of them catching us?" asked George Heritage.

He spoke in careful, hesitant Spanish, the only kind he knew.

"The *Hina?* Ah, *señor,* she has been many a time in such scrapes!"

Lopez (if that was his name — which George doubted)

spoke in an English that could be placed alongside of George Heritage's Spanish, schoolbookishly correct. He was a slim lad of sixteen or seventeen, fussy, and a shade effeminate.

"I suppose so."

"Maybe she has already run from this boat. They knew her."

"Yes, everybody knows her, except me. I reckon she's the most notorious gunrunner in the West Indies. But me, I come from Maine. I didn't ask enough questions. I thought I was being hired as a demolition expert. I thought they'd booked me and my dynamite to show 'em how to blast stumps out of land that was needed for planting. I really did think that. Cross my heart."

The boy put a hand on George's arm. It was like the hand of a woman, so sharply and small.

"Ah, *señor*, you should not feel ashamed of innocence! To be innocent, they say, is to be a poet!"

"Well, I don't happen to want to be a poet. All I want is to make a living. And revolutions are no place for that."

"*Señor*, when you have seen my land you will feel different."

Unabashed, he tightened his grip on Geroge's arm, and when he looked up it was with eyes wet and bright with tears. They were dark-brown eyes, almond-shaped, in certain lights flecked with gold.

George looked at him, thinking: *Hell, when I was that age I wouldn't have let anybody see me bawling.*

"*Cuba libre means that much to you, then?*"

"*Cuba libre* means everything to me!"

Somebody shouted something, and they looked up to see a gunner working the plug out of the muzzle of the coast guard boat's bow-chaser. In a moment there was a long orange-red flash at that muzzle, and smoke fluttered back like some hag in a gray shawl shrugging her shoulders. The shell kicked up a spear of water at least two hundred yards astern of them.

Cupping his hands, the boy lit a cigarette. It disgusted George Heritage, who, until he came south, had thought that only pimps smoked those things.

"But they would not wish to hit us even if they could, so long as they had a chance of catching us. Why kill us all at once, with nobody watching?"

George scowled.

"Oh, come now! This is the nineteenth century!"

The year, in fact, was 1895. The month was May.

"They don't know that in Madrid," the boy replied.

Yet Lopez showed no nervousness as he stared back at the coast guard boat. The little sailors in white who tended the gun made no further movement; but neither was the plug, the tampion, replaced.

"She won't get us," Lopez said at last. "But all the same, it might be well to set one's soul at rest. If you will excuse me, *señor* . . ."

He actually bowed.

"Why, I always excuse people who want to say their prayers!"

The boy took it seriously.

"That is kind of you, *señor*," he said; and he threw away his cigarette, and bowed again, and went below.

George Heritage looked around, sardonic, bemused; nevertheless, he was impressed. Whatever else they might be, these men weren't cowards. Classically, he supposed, there was always something of the comic opera about a Latin-American revolution. He should have been laughing. He had never felt less like it.

The scene to shoreward in truth was unreal, hard to believe. The water was too blue to be wet, the coastguard boat too pretty to be effective, while the hills of Cuba might have been a wallpaper motif in some nursery. All the same, the chase, if quiet, was tense. Nobody around George belittled it. The brass piece from this distance *did* suggest a toy; but it had spoken once, and could speak again. The distance between the two boats was slowly but

7

unquestionably increasing; yet nobody gloated, nobody gave a cheer. There were eight passengers aboard the *Hina,* including George Heritage, and all of these, excepting young Lopez, were on deck now, together with both hands, the mate, and the captain—all of the crew but two engineers and two stokers. There was not much talk.

One man shrugged and, like Lopez, threw his cigarette overboard and went below. Another followed him. The skipper sent the mate to the engine room.

"It will be a long day, *señor.* May the saints decree that we see the end of it."

"Mañana sera otra dia," tried George.

"True. Oh, sure."

This was one of the deck hands, a stubby small man with a red face mottled with little tufts of whisker that seemed stuck into it like cloves in a baked ham. His English was fluent, if coarse. His eyes had a vulpine brightness; his nose was venous and very fat. George could not remember his name — it sounded like a sneeze anyway — but thought of him, and sometimes addressed him, as Pedro.

"Would they really execute somebody if they overtook us?"

"Señor, they would kill every one. They'd call us pirates."

"They can't do that!"

"You are a norteamericano. You don't know what things are done these days in Cuba." He nodded to the shore, clearer now. "If I could swim, I wouldn't wait to see."

"You're a sailor and you can't swim?"

Pedro only gazed morosely at the coast guard boat.

"I know few sailors who can swim, *señor.* But — you?"

"Oh, yes."

"That far?"

"I guess so. In fact, I'm sure I could."

"Then I'd advise you to."

"Horse apples! I'm a U. S. citizen!"

"So are many of us. We have passports. But officers don't

always believe such documents. So many of them these days are forgeries."

"Mine's genuine. I'm a real U. S. citizen, born in Maine. Why, there have been Heritages in Androscoggin County for almost two hundred years — ever since there *was* an Androscoggin County."

Pedro fetched a sigh.

"All the same, I would swim it if I could," he said.

"And run the risk of sharks?"

"*Señor*," the little man whispered, "better a shark than a Spaniard!"

There was a clatter from the engine room. The tug's convulsive shuddering all but ceased: it was an abrupt as any explosion might have been. She yawed crazily, and steam shrieked through the 'scape pipes. Speed fell off so suddenly that it seemed as though the deck had been jerked like a rug under their feet.

None of the revolutionists moved, except to take the cigars or cigarettes out of their mouths and swivel their eyes toward the skipper, who held the wheel.

The mate fairly burst out of the engine room. He gabbled to the skipper. Because of the steam in the 'scape pipes, most of the men on deck could not hear all the words, but there was something about a broken piston.

"In God's hands," one of them said gently, as though to himself. "Well, where else have we ever been?"

The skipper spun the wheel, and *Hina*, seeming almost to exhale in relief, turned toward the shore.

She would never make it.

The coast guard boat moved a few points to starboard, intent upon cutting them off.

The hatch was ripped open, but the cases it contained were not easily budged. They were long heavy cases, coffin-shaped, each stamped *Oliver Chilled Plows.*

Everybody was working now, wildly, furiously.

The case containing George Heritage's dynamite was one of the first to come out. It had been stored on top, despite

9

George's earnest assurance that there was no slight chance of spontaneous combustion or any other accidental discharge. It was heavier than the others, which contained Springfield rifles; and once they had hoisted it to the deck they ignored it, to work upon the lighter cases.

They got one of those over the rail. Then they got a second one over.

The brass piece coughed, and the splash this time was very close . . . and a little forward.

They got a third case overboard.

The coast guard boat, slackening speed, came alongside, only a few yards away, between the tug and the shore. Her rail was lined with men who carried carbines. Her brass bow-chaser and a Lowell repeater on her afterdeck were pointed at the *Hina*.

"*Señor*," Pedro panted, "you should have jumped."

CHAPTER II

THE PRIEST had the purple-scarlet complexion of an English foxhunting squire. His reddish hair might have been Scandinavian. He was tall, young, lank, and badly scared. His lips moved constantly. As he went from man to man, it was with the walk of one who wades through hip-deep water. His eyes, light blue, wobbled back and forth. Tears flooded them, broke, and zig-zagged down his cheeks.

When the first volley was heard, just outside of the prison, not fifty feet feet from where the men were chained, it seemed to strike the priest like a fist, He stopped, and even staggered, stunned; but he recovered, to make the circuit of the dungeon once again, droning on, holding up his crucifix.

The volley meant that four men were dead.

There had been sixteen—eight passengers, eight sailors—every one of whom, after a fifty-minute hearing before seven Spanish officers the previous afternoon, had been convicted of piracy. They were to be killed at dawn, in fours.

Most of the men had taken this with no more than a moan, their heads hung. They were fatalists.

Not so George Heritage. George was not sure where this town of Purisima Concepcion was, but he did know that it was near Santiago-de-Cuba, and there must be a U. S. consul at Santiago. Didn't the Ward Line put in there?

George had insisted upon the right to consult that consul, and had been coldly refused.

There had been no gratuitious insult. Nobody had spit in anybody's face. The passports—four sailors, among them Pedro, had claimed U. S. citizenship—had not been torn up, only shoved aside. The defendants had been asked, individually, if they had anything to say for themselves. Most of them shook their heads. A few, chins high, had made brief patriotic speeches, ending with shout. "Cuba libre!" Only George had stooped to plead for his life.

Concentrating upon the president of the court, a colonel with dead-mackerel eyes and a scarlet coat upon which gleamed the green-ribboned Cross of Calatrava, George had held forth about the blood lines of his family, naming members of it as far back as four generations. This part of the discourse alone seemed to interest a few of the officers, and they had leaned forward a little; but the colonel never stirred.

Speaking sometimes in Spanish but sometimes, when he got excited, in English, George had explained the nature of his own training and his profession. He had related the tale of his embarkment aboard the tug at Tampa, asserting that he had supposed himself hired to aid in a campaign of plantation expansion in Oriente Province. He added that not until the *Hina* was at sea had he learned that he was with gunrunners. He had admitted that the largest packing case in the hold bore his name, was assigned to him, and in fact was his property. He had conceded that its contents consisted of 350 pounds of well-calcined Kieselguhr, an infusorial earth, saturated with pure nitroglycerine, but with all the vehemence at his command he had insisted that dynamite was not simply a military material.

"Even when it's being smuggled into a country at war?"

"Señor, your own government had told the world that there is not a state of war in Cuba, only an unseemly brawl."

"Hmm. . . ."

12

"Dynamite is used to blast railroad cuts and tunnels. It is used to open coal mines."

"And . . . here?"

"Tree stumps."

For the first and only time the colonel had almost smiled; and George, humiliated, had raged on. He had denied that he knew the case of dynamite was stenciled *"Oliver Chilled Plows."* He had demanded again that he be permitted to see the consul at Santiago.

There had been no retirement, or formal vote. The colonel had but glanced negligently at his colleagues, one after the other; and each had lowered his head a bit, for an instant closing his eyes. Then they signed the condemnation, which had been made out in advance. And the prisoners were led back to their cell.

For they were all in one room, a square, stone chamber, low-roofed, gloomy. The only light, like the only air, came through a grated door, there being no window. Around the walls, firmly set into the stone, about head-high, were eight rings of iron. Through each ring ran a steel chain about three feet long, each end of which held a pair of handcuffs. Thus it was that the sixteen men were manacled, standing, facing a glum wet wall.

They had been that way for thirteen hours, with no exercise, nothing to eat or drink. It was only at the expense of strain both for himself and his chain-companion that one of them could even turn around; and when he did there was nothing for him to see but the backs of his fellow prisoners and the pail in the middle of the room.

Of course none of them could reach the pail, and when it was necessary for him to relieve himself he had to call the jailer, who would unlock him for a little while. The jailer, though asked to, never had emptied the pail, which now was about three-quarters full. The air was stench-ridden.

It was an ignominious way to spend your last hours on earth.

13

After the volley there was a sound of gun butts being grounded, but no crack of a *coup de grace;* there was, instead, a faint but full sigh like an "amen."

Next to George, on his right, the side toward the door, stood the boy Lopez. He was not praying, though he had prayed before. Eyes closed, stolidly he faced the wall, his hands raised to the ring in order to give his chain-companion a chance to kneel. That companion was a man at least twice the lad's age and much bigger of frame; yet he sagged, exhausted, only partly conscious, while the boy remained erect. He was the eighth in line from the door, counting from left to right, as the sergeant had counted when he ordered the gyves struck from the wrists of the first four; that is, Lopez would be in the second squad of death. George Heritage, the ninth man, would be the first of the third squad. It was all very neat.

"Psst!"

This was Pedro, on the other side, the tenth man, with whom George shared a chain, a ring. Pedro pressed something into George's hands. It was a pint flask, made of glass, corked, with no label.

"Rum. Drink it. It has been passed around."

George Heritage liked a little whiskey now and then, but he was not fond of rum. Nevertheless, he was furiously thirsty. He glanced sideways at Lopez, wondering . . .

"No, no! He had had his. It started from him."

"I see."

He drank the rum, tipping the flask high. It was scarcely enough to wet the top of his tongue.

There was a scuffling. The Spanish soldiers wore canvas shoes with rope soles. The door was thrown open.

It seemed barbarously abrupt. Shouldn't they have waited, at least for a little while? There could hardly have been time to clear away the bodies. Perhaps they were nervous out there?

"I want to use the pail," cried George Heritage.

There was a murmur of disapproval, and even the soldiers

14

looked shocked that a prisoner should think of his own comfort at a time like this, delaying death for his comrades. But George repeated his demand.

The sergeant growled a refusal, but he changed his mind. After all, death does have its dignity, and a man who is about to go should be indulged a little. Besides, as head of the squad, the sergeant was at least partially responsible for the appearance of the prisoners, who would be gawped at by a crowd. So he gave a nod.

"Don't be long, though."

"I won't," George promised, and went to the pail, turning his back on the soldiers.

Half a minute later he was again chained to Pedro, while the four men to his right were being released.

Nobody wept. But as the men filed through the doorway there came from those who were left a susurrant murmur, "Adios." That was all. And the door was swung shut, the feet shuffled away.

The Spaniards used Mausers. To those in the cell, the clack of the bolts being thrown as cartridges were pumped into the barrels was a loud startling sound. That must have been a large firing squad out there—a dozen men? Sixteen?

The pause that followed was excruciating No noise could be heard, no moving-about, nor officers' commands. The silence seemed to extend for minutes . . . minutes . . .

The crash, though they had been waiting for it, praying for it, jolted them.

It was followed by another of those underbreath "amens."

Then the sound of the rope-soled shoes again. The door was thrown open. The sergeant came in. He pointed to George Heritage.

"All right. You next."

15

CHAPTER III

The sunlight clubbed him. He had supposed that he was about to step forth into a slate-gray dawn, one bleak and chilly. Instead he was drenched in brilliance.

Then, when his vision had cleared, he was to regret this. Fleetingly he wished that he had been born blind. A blind person would know only by hearsay what butchers his fellow men could be.

Something—the stock of a Mauser?—struck him in the small of the back, causing him to lurch forward.

This was not a walled yard but a paved open space, that faced away from the sea, toward the hills. It was level for perhaps a hundred yards, and after that, sloping sharply upward, was stippled with boulders and with careless nodding palms. There were no lanes or even paths.

Higher, as though it was tumbling down this hill and had been but momentarily checked, was the forest.

There were perhaps two hundred soldiers drawn up in two files that formed three sides of a square, the open side being the one toward the hills. There were at least twice that many civilians.

Facing the open space, their backs to the prison, were the officers. Except that they were standing, they might have been in session as a court martial again: they were ranged in the same order. The colonel stood with his dirty-window-pane mustaches, his Cross of Calatrava, in the middle; the

16

others were on either side; behind them stood the junior officers and clerks and the interpreter.

Some fifty feet from these officers, beyond the paved space, forming a fourth side of the square, a long ditch had been dug. The fresh earth was piled on the far side of this ditch, toward the hill.

Four men had been kneeling at the edge of the ditch. They knelt no longer, but were flat on their faces, their wrists still fastened behind them. One had slithered halfway into the ditch, and only his legs protruded. The back of each—for they had not been permitted to face their executioners—was a mass of shredded shirt, ripped flesh and blood.

Flies already hummed around each of those smashed, pulpy backs. The buzzards, more wary, flumped in wide, low circles just above, their skinny necks outstretched.

"Over there," a voice behind George said. "They'll tie your arms."

A soldier shoved the legs of the half-seen body into the ditch so that it disappeared altogether. Other soldiers were dragging the other bodies across the ground. One became sick and paused. He was hardly more than a boy,—of the same age as the corpse he dragged, Lopez—and his face, dead pale, was wet with sweat. An officer swore at him, and he resumed his task.

"If you don't get over there—"

George moved swiftly. He started toward the man with the bonds, but stopped, turning to face the colonel.

"Do you know what's in this?"

He whipped the rum flask from under his shirt and held it high. It was filled with a clear liquid, light yellow in color.

"This is nitroglycerine!"

He did not know the Spanish for his two important words, and said them in English. But the effect was all he had hoped for. He was understood. Up and down the line he could hear men gasp *"dinamita,"* and, better, *"nitroglicerina."*

The whole world seemed to stand on tiptoe, breathless. There was no voices, no footstep. The company was paralyzed. Wildly, George fancied that even the flies at the dead men's backs, even the wheeling lumbrous buzzards, had paused, frozen in midair, as though by some charm. He did not look around. He did not move even his eyes, for he continued to glare at the colonel.

"I brought it because I wanted to impregnate some charcoal made from cork. They say it makes good dynamite, and I wanted to find out for myself. And you have cork trees here, see?"

The colonel did not so much as twitch. His eyes were coated with contempt, his mouth was fixed in a disdainful leer.

"If the *señor* . . ."

His voice was unexpectedly soft, placating. Plainly he thought himself confronted by a madman.

"The *señor* will not! God damn you all, if I've got to go I'll go my own way! *Cuba libre!*"

George threw the flask high into the air.

He did not see it smash, though he heard it, as he heard at the same time screams and the thump of men who fell, fainting. George already had whirled around, grabbed Pedro's arm, and started to sprint toward the ditch.

Pedro grinned, all teeth.

"I was ready, *señor*. I saw you fill that bottle, at the pail."

"Don't talk! *Run!*"

They sped past the spot where, minutes before, the men had knelt. The blood, drying at the edges, crisping brown, had not yet soaked into the earth.

They leapt across the ditch and its gruesome holding.

Pedro, the shorter, barely made the far side, where he wavered, squealing, waving his arms to regain his balance. George hauled him to safety.

They screamed up that parapet of loose earth, which crumbled under hands, feet, knees.

Not until they had reached the top of this did they hear shots. These were scattered and curiously hollow, like so many doors being slammed in an empty house.

Cascading dirt and stones, they slid to the far side.

The muscular pain as they rose was almost unbearable. They'd been standing in one spot for thirteen hours.

They clenched their teeth; they lowered their heads—and ran!

The way was steep now. It was strewn with rocks. They looked neither to right nor to left, neither behind nor ahead, but labored on as though against some unseen, supernatural force.

How far was the forest? They had been running for a long time. Pedro, a fat little man with stubby legs, older than George, kept falling back.

"You . . . go . . . on!"

"Shut up!"

When the shooting started again behind them, it seemed exceedingly far away, a thin pip-pip-pip; but it grew close, and they heard with it the clip clop of hooves.

For the first time, George looked back.

Five horsemen were riding up the slope. One, a smallish man in white, was well ahead of the rest. Even as George looked, this man rose in his stirrups and put his carbine to his shoulder and fired.

It had been a lucky shot, and the man in white could scarcely believe it. Before he could spur on, exultant, the others had caught up with him. They came in a row, spread out, waving their guns.

George knelt beside Pedro and turned him over. Pedro's eyes were glazed. He tired to say something but blood gushed out of his mouth. Feebly he shook his head. With failing sight, he indicated the edge of the forest: George should run for it.

George tried to lift him. Impossible. He tried to drag him.

Pedro went on shaking his head. The fountain of blood was ceaseless. How could one man hold so much of the stuff?

Then his eyes rolled up and he ceased even to shake his head.

Sobbing, George ran for the trees. The hoofbeats were right behind him.

He fairly threw himself into the cover. It was like a man whose clothes were afire diving into a pool. The immediate sensation, indeed, was somewhat similar. The air must have been twenty degrees cooler in the shade of those trees; and to him, his body drenched with sweat, it was like an ice-water douche.

He lay still, heart beating violently. He could see along the hillside, which hurt his eyes. He could see the prison, and the men running around down there. He could see the horsemen, who had reined to a stop within a few feet of where he lay; but he did not believe that they could see him, swathed in shadows as he was. They looked right down at him, but they shook their heads. It was as though they had been playing a child's game; once the fugitive made that tree line he was to be considered "home." They glanced at one another and shrugged; then they turned.

Now George could see Pedro, spread-eagled on the ground. He must be dead! The Spaniards rode back to him and dismounted. One kicked Pedro's head, with no result. Another placed the muzzle of his carbine, a Winchester repeater, within an inch of Pedro's right eye. He giggled. He pulled the trigger.

The impact of the bullet jolted Pedro's head. It looked as though the corpse was still trying to say "no."

The men heaved what was left of that tubby little sailor across the hind quarters of the largest horse, his legs dangling on one side, his arms on the other. Then they rode down the hill, laughing and talking. The buzzards were gathering around them, wheeling low, their skinny necks protruding, their little red eyes avid.

Those buzzards were the last things George was to see for some hours.

CHAPTER IV

WHEN HE AWOKE the sun was low, the slope was smeared with crimson, and the tiny figures of soldiers at the fort shone as though they had been enameled.

He lay motionless, afraid to move, while his groggy mind cleared.

The town of Purisima Concepcion might have been asleep. No person moved there, not even a dog. The white walls soaked up what was left of the sunshine, while the bay beyond, an unbelievable blue, basked in those last rays. The coast guard boat had gone.

There was nothing to mark the spot where Pedro had fallen; but the fresh big grave, down below, was bulgingly clear. No markers had been erected upon it. No priest had prayed there, no townsman gazed with wondering eyes upon the burial place.

George fetched a sigh that seared his lungs.

Comic opera, eh?

He cursed himself. The hard-headed Down Easterner! The fifth-generation Yankee! He had driven a sharp bargain, as he fondly supposed, when approached by members of the Boston branch of the Friends of Cuba, disguised for this occasion as representatives of a planters' syndicate. He had put a high price on his services, congratulating himself when those naive islanders hastened to accept. He had paid for his own passage by sea to Jacksonville; then, checking his 350 pounds of dynamite as personal baggage, he had gone,

21

again at his own expense, by that miserable, dirty, slow railroad to Tampa.

Not a penny had he been paid, even after he learned that he was among blockade runners. He didn't have so much as a return ticket. A fistfull of Uncle Sam's cash, he fancied, might come in handy to a bush fugitive; but the jailor at Purisima Concepcion had cleaned him out.

He had nothing to fight with, nothing to bribe with. He scarcely knew the language. He was not even sure where he was.

He must move with care—but move he *must!* The large, low, dark-red sun warned him of night. He had heard that in the tropics there was no dusk, no wavering twilight. It was like the turning-off of a gas jet.

Besides, he was cold. Had not his eyes told him, when he looked out upon the town, that he was on a hillside, he might have supposed himself in a swamp. He twitched, and his teeth chattered like castanets.

Gingerly wincing, he rose. He began to cast about.

He soon saw why his pursuers had broken off their pursuit. They had not, of course, known that he was too weak to run any further; but they would have been obliged to enter the forest on foot, so thick was the underbrush. Even then, spread out, fumbling, they might have lost one another before they found him.

George Heritage always had been at home in the woods, but this was not Maine.

He couldn't see his feet which alternately were stuck in gluelike mud or went slithering this way and that. Spiked creepers scratched his skin, tore his clothes. Wet spongy hanks of Spanish moss caressed him, falling like curtains behind him.

He went faster and faster, until he was fairly running. Again and again he slipped and fell, but he rose in frantic haste to speed on. He caught his feet in roots, was slapped by swaying ropelike lianas collided with trees, but he kept on going.

Suddenly he stopped, hearing only his own half-strangled breath. That a man brought up in Androscoggin County should behave like this! Yet what else could he do? No dribble of daylight reached him, and he had no idea in which direction Purisima Concepcion lay. His lore would not help him here. In Maine the moss usually was thickest on the north side of the trees; but here the only moss was Spanish moss, long stifling hanks of it hanging from the limbs of trees. Even if he had known how the prevailing winds blew in this part of the world, there was no stir of air. The moon and stars? He could not even see the sky.

Desperate, he was about to resort to something he'd been told was the worst possible tactic for one who is lost in the woods; that is, he was about to start casting around in a large circle, always increasing its size in the wild hope that sooner or later he would have to come upon *something* he knew by sight or by feel. Sanity, however, prevailed, and a better plan presented itself.

After all, he reasoned, he was on a hillside. The slope might not be as steep as it had seemed when, with pain-racked limbs and Pedro beside him, he scaled it; but he knew, having seen it before his break for freedom, that this was plateau he stood on, but a continuing forest that stretched some distance to the very top of the row of hills. Therefore if he went *down,* he would assuredly come out once more upon the plain.

It should have been absurdly simple, to learn which way was *down.* It turned out to be very difficult indeed. He had nothing to squint along, nothing to drop, to see it roll.

This was absurd! He held out his arms like a man who walks a tight-rope. He tottered on the balls of his feet.

At last though by no means sure of himself, he determined upon a direction and resolutely marched that way.

Almost at once he came out of the forest.

He saw now that he could not have counted upon getting a glimpse of daylight, for the sun already had set. The moon had not yet risen, though stars were tumbling out. The stars, however, were arranged in a pattern that was not familiar: it gave George Heritage an added feeling of uneasiness to reflect that even the stars were not in their right places. What *could* he trust?

He had not eaten a crumb since the pre-dawn breakfast aboard of *Hina* the previous morning, forty-odd hours ago, and his hunger, acute now, was like a cramp, doubling him over.

There were some lights at the prison, but he could see nothing to mark a scouting party. The town was dark. Not a boat be seen in the bay.

For a wild instant, as he emerged from the wood, he thought that the plain was swarming with men who smoked cigars. But these were fireflies, hundreds of them, thousands, each by far the biggest George ever had seen. They flitted very low.

He was prepared to eat or drink anything he could get, but self-preservation is a strong instinct. He would have to keep away from the town, if possible never moving far from the forest.

So he sidled crabwise down the slope, facing the sea, his back to the trees.

Soon the moon appeared, and he was able to discern a path beneath his feet, a path into which he must have walked by chance.

He began to see huts. It was not extraordinary that he had missed these previously, for they were scattered and appeared to blend into the terrain. They were small, ten or fifteen feet across, round, high, made of some sort of thatch, pointed on top. They were strewn haphazardly across the plain.

No smoke rose from any of these huts, and not one showed any light; indeed, they did not appear to have windows.

What was worse, neither did they seem to have pigpens, chicken runs, cabbage patches or apple orchards. George could not even see a hay rick to sleep in.

He passed several of these huts at some distance. Then, when he found himself approaching one directly, he determined to knock. Even if they reported him, they might give him something to eat first.

"Quien vive?"

He stopped, for the voice had a commanding, whiplike rap.

"Now, look . . ." he started. "I only wondered if you—"

The flash of flame, a bit to the right of the doorway, was unmistakable, as was the slam of the shot itself. It was not a crack, as of a rifle, but rather a hollow, hoarse, coughing sound such as might have been made by an old-fashioned musket.

George ducked, spinning. He made for the forest. But he heard no sound of alarm, and in a little while he edged down the slope again.

He glanced toward the fort. Had they heard that shot down there? What breeze there was was off the bay. He saw no stir at all.

Had he not been so hungry and thirsty, he would have retreated to the forest to sleep as best he could. But he had to have food.

He squared his shoulders and started for the nearest thatched hut. He did not walk aggressively, but neither did he slink. For he believed, despite the silence, that he was being watched.

He knocked at the door and waited. He thought that he could hear somebody breathing. He knocked again, harder.

At last, he heard a quavering voice saying, *"Quien va?"*

George noted instantly that this man had cried *"Quien va?"*—"Who goes?"—whereas the other, the one who had shot at him, had called *"Quien vive?"* or "Who lives?" He did not ponder this point, but started to talk in a low, earnest, hurried voice. He didn't beg for shelter, only for food and water. He said he was dying.

"Uno minuto . . ."

There was a scraping of thatch and, as though by magic,

a pair of hands appeared through the wall. Each hand cupped half a coconut.

"God bless you, man!"

"Sh-sh! For the love of the saints, *señor*, go far away from here to eat and drink it. And don't come back! Oh, please!"

"I will," George promised.

He didn't. He was too hungry. He squatted right there, first emptying each of the half-coconuts of its liquid, then with eager fingers tearing out chunks of the meat. The milk was rancid and almost made him sick, but the meat was sweet.

"Señor, in the name of . . . *Don't you see them?"*

He saw men coming out of the fort. There was no blare of bugles, no clank of arms, but parties were being formed, were spread out. Already some of them starting up the hillside. That shot had been heard after all.

"I'm sorry," he muttered, meaning it. "If they catch me I won't say you gave me this no matter what they do to me. Thanks again."

He had no trouble regaining the shadow of the forest. There, crouching, shivering, he ate the rest of the coconut.

The world was hurting him everywhere. He throbbed. He got his back against a tree and pulled his knees up. He might have slept a bit. He would never know. *Pink* was his first sensory realization. Alarmed, but bewildered, he popped his eyes fully open and perceived that it was not pink at all but a virulent red.

Something was burning!

The light that flared against all manner of strange fronds and creepers and leaves around and above him came from his right. He crept to the edge of the forest.

It might have been a giant's bonfire. The flames, upreaching, waved wildly, while a column of sparks flew upward.

The native whose hut was being burned could hardly have enjoyed this glorious sight.

George watched it for a long while, as long as it lasted.

That stuff ignites quickly and burns very fast. Soon there was nothing left but a bed of sullenly glowing ashes.

The power of Spain had spoken.

George could only hope that the hut had been casually picked. He could hope that it hadn't been the home of the man who had given him the coconut.

He could only hope . . .

If he survived he would never hunt again. He thought he knew now how the animal felt. The big game were truly hunted. They were *stalked;* and George now knew what it was like to be stalked.

This might have been his imagination. Conceivably nobody was even thinking about him. They could have stricken his name off the record; to keep things tidy, they could have framed a report that simply set down sixteen executions. Military men, he had been told, sometimes did things like that.

But he was frightened. The hand of every man, of every living thing, he thought, was against him. He started at each small sound. His eyes ached from their ceaseless rotation.

He had spent many a night in the open, but never one like this. He thought it would never end. Sometimes he sat with his back against a tree, or even lay full-length, but he got little sleep. Mostly he walked along the edge of the plain, prepared to spring back into the forest at any sound or movement. He was in an agony of apprehension, all nerves.

With the dawn he got a better grip on himself. Yet daylight was to limit his movements. There was a stir down in Purisima Concepcion. Mules were driven, chickens fed, sentries relieved.

He studied the situation.

Though there was a great deal of movement in and around the fort, there was nothing to indicate that he, George Heritage, was the cause of it. Officers were not passing from house to house to ask if anything had been seen of the escaped man. As for the hut that had been burned, perhaps this was too common a sight, it drew no crowd.

The forest, though dense wtih undergrowth, was, when you could see it, not a bad place. He cast about, his ears open for the sound of water, until he located a cool small brook.

Most of the trees on the slopes were the tall straight palms called royal palms, but some were coconut trees. Beneath these were many nuts—his, he assumed, for the taking. Today all he could do was longingly eye them.

He did find many small, hard, dark-red berries, not unlike the berries on the holly folks at home used to hang in their windows at Christmas time. He chewed a few, then more; but he resisted the temptation to cram a whole handful into his mouth, for he feared that they would make him sick. The berries were too hard to get down; therefore he ground juice out of them and spat the pulp. The juice was bitter, but it did help to quiet his wobbly stomach.

He saw that the forest was not as wild as he had supposed. There were paths which appeared to be well traveled. There were cuttings, clearings, where woodsmen had been at work, charcoal makers probably. He avoided these.

The cardinal directions were clear to him now, thanks to the sun. He did not know, however, whether this part of the southern coast of Cuba was east or west of Santiago. His purpose was to get, somehow, to that U. S. consul. Every mile would be paved with pain, and a start the wrong way might cost him his life. Again *should* he cling to the coast? Wouldn't they expect him to do that? He had heard that a good part of Oriente Province, the eastern third of the island of Cuba, was in rebel hands, with the Spaniards controlling only the cities, towns, forts, railroads and harbors. If this were true, might not George's best move to be a retreat into the interior, where the natives would be less frightened? Perhaps he could pick out a large house and go to it; then throw himself on the mercy of its master. He had nothing to hide. He would ask only for a means of conveyance to Santiago and direc-

28

tions how to get there. What humane person could refuse this?

He noted that most of the traffic into and out of Purisima Concepcion was along a shore road that went west. This could mean that either Santiago or some large town was in that direction, or else that there was a road that led through a gap in the hills to the hinterland.

The latter was the case, as he was to learn in the middle of the afternoon. There was a fold in the hills, a very decided one, down the middle of which a stream meandered. The shore road turned at this point, thereafter to go north. It was a narrow road, very dusty, not bordered by any hedge, fence, or ditch. George would not venture upon it until after sundown.

He found some more berries and sat down to watch and to wait.

When he did quit the forest it was gingerly. He believed that the military had imposed a curfew upon this countryside, for he had noticed that the late afternoon travelers quickened their steps in a most unCuban manner, anxiously regarding the sun. In that even there would be no civilian travel at night; but there might be military patrols.

He walked quickly, at all times watching the ground on either side of the road, turning occasionally to look behind him. Twice he did duck into cover, once behind a boulder, once behind a snake fence, while a pair of horsemen passed. It might have been the same pair each time. There was no moon, and he could not be sure.

On another occasion his eye was caught by a wide-spreading, low-branched tree which, on examination, proved to hold fruit. It was easy to pick these fruits without climbing. They were green and shiny, each somewhat like a pear in shape, though twice as big as any pear. George never had seen anything like them. He cut one open with a sharp stone and saw that it contained a large, almond-shaped pit surrounded by reddish pulpy meat. He tasted the meat. It was delicious.

29

Nevertheless he made good speed, with long strides, dust spiraling from around his feet. The sky, a dark, disagreeable blue washed with stars, held itself aloof.

He reckoned that it was somewhat past midnight, and that he had traveled at least twelve or thirteen miles from the coast, when he saw the light. He had passed huts, yet each was dark. But the light, he saw at last, was from a window, a fairly high window—obviously a large house. It was well back from the road, up a lane lined wtih hibiscus bushes.

Unhesitatingly George turned into that lane.

Then his step slowed. Unsure of his Spanish, he was equally unsure of his welcome. There was war in this land, so there would be marauders. He might be fired upon.

There was a stirring a little ahead, in a bush.

He stopped, stiffening.

A shadow hurtled out of that bush and came straight for George. Two arms were thrown around his neck.

"Caro mio! O, mi corazon!"

"Well, I'll be damned," muttered George Heritage.

He was holding in his arms the most beautiful woman he had ever seen.

CHAPTER VI

GEORGE HERITAGE was one of those men, who, when they wake up, wake up all over. He did not trail wisps of slumber behind him.

His third morning in Cuba made up an exception. His eyes throbbed, his limbs were lead, his stomach a mass of pain.

He was between linen sheets.

After what he had been through, it would be extraordinary, he supposed, if he did not suffer from fatigue. Yet he resented it. By nature he was almost offensively healthy; his was the arrogance of an athlete; his body had never failed to do what he asked of it.

He propped himself on one elbow, to gaze with bleary eyes out of a window by his side. He began to chuckle, for he had never seen anything so funny as those trees out there. They were not tall, and they were laid out in rows, so it was clear that they had been cultivated. Rubber? Bananas? The leaves were in wise notable, being large, smooth, glossy, oblong; but the fruit consisted of purplish-yellow protuberances perhaps eight or nine inches long. The fruit seemed to grow right out of the trunk of each tree, which gave it the ludicrous look of something fastened there, say, with a piece of wire.

"Buenos dias, señor."

Now here was another funny-looking thing: short, squat, ineffably amiable. He reminded George of Pedro, a born

31

clown. His hair helter-skeltered all over his head. His teeth gleamed.

He put a tray on the edge of the bed.

"I am Manuelo," he said shyly.

"Thank you, Manuelo." George pointed to the tray. "What's that?"

"Chocolate. Mango."

The chocolate George had recognized. The mango he now saw was the same fruit that he had eaten by the side of the road.

He pointed out the window.

"What's *that?*"

"Cuba, *señor*." ·

"No, no, the trees!"

He made motions with his hands.

"Oh," cried Manuelo, catching on, beaming. "Cacao. Like that." He pointed to the cup.

"Oh, cocoa."

"Cacao."

"So that's what it looks like?"

"There are not many such in Cuba, *señor*. My master, Don Diego, he brought them from Nicaragua. He tries them out."

"I see. Your master's a very fine gentleman, Manuelo."

"My master is a saint."

"Well put. Now if I may be alone for a little while . . ."

Fully awake now, he tried to think of Don Diego, in order to keep from thinking of Don Diego's daughter.

Never had George known such a greeting, and he was warmed and humbled by the memory.

The girl's face had been not only lovely in itself but also curiously, and bafflingly, familiar. He had scarcely more than glimpsed it out there in the lane, for as soon as she saw who he was she fled to the house.

When nothing happened he had started again for the light. He had called, "Hello there! Is anybody home?" A door was opened, and he saw Diego Pineda for the first time in silhouette, a tall man, rail-thing, erect. George was challenged, first in Spanish, then in deliberate English. He had said bluntly that he was hungry, thirsty, and so tired that he could scarcely stand. The man in the doorway never hesitated. Unfearful of a trap, he had hurried out to George, had guided him indoors. *"Su casa,"* he'd said. "Your house."

A servant had been summoned, a female, an Indian with the face of a disconsolate shad. Wine and meat and fruit and a wash basin were produced. Later there were cigars and brandy.

Ceremoniously Don Diego, who had already introduced himself, introduced his daughter, the Señorita Ana.

She had come from upstairs. She made a patterned curtsey, never lifting her eyes George bowed, deciding that he too would say nothing of the kiss in the lane.

He was sure that he'd never seen this young woman before, yet he must have seen her likeness. Did she resemble some famous portrait?

Still without looking up, she murmured a few words of greeting.

"Ana," her father said profoundly, "speaks English well "

She had said nothing more, and when Don Diego dismissed her with a graceful wave of the hand, she departed without a sound, it being as though a shadow had gone because the light was moved.

"It is with regret that I do not have my son Mateo to greet you also, *señor*. He studies in New York, the school called Columbia."

"Went to Bowdoin myself," George muttered.

For some time after that, gravely yet with a touching warmth, Don Diego had talked about his son. George had hardly listened. George had been thinking about the Señorita Ana.

He couldn't know the color of her eyes, having been given no chance to see them in the candlelight. Her hair, too, had been hidden, but she had cameo-perfect features set in a small face, and her skin suggested ivory.

She was no slip of a girl, though she was short. Despite

33

the downcast eyes, the careful, subdued manners, and though she held a shawl around her, he saw that her bosom rose and fell.

Not the least fascinating thing about the Señorita Ana was that she could stand in that hall, so demure, so obedient, all rectitude, when only a few minutes before she had waylaid a lover and pressed him in passionate embrace.

It might pay, George reflected, to get to know such a person.

But now he tried to think of Don Diego.

The host, with exquisite taste, had refused to listen to George's story, pointing out that George was tired. The tale could wait, Don Diego had said.

Don Diego, however, had a right to know. He had taken in the wayfarer, and fed and rested him. It was possible that this act of charity would get him into trouble. At the very least he should be warned, as George had tried to warn him last night.

He got out of bed—and reeled. This infuriated him. He, George Heritage of Androscoggin County, had been obliged to seize a bedpost in order to stand up. It was outrageous!

He straightened carefully, like a self-conscious drunkard, and walked around the room several times before starting to shave.

When he went downstairs he felt somewhat steadier, though his stomach still ached, his face was hot, his mouth aflame.

The shad-faced Indian nodded toward a terrace, and George went outside to meet his host.

Don Diego asked if he had slept well, if he had had breakfast? That Manuelo was lazy scamp who must be watched.

"Now, first I've got to tell you how I got here—"

"If it hurts you, *señor*—"

"No, no! You must hear about it!"

Don Diego listened gravely, sometimes shaking his head, sometimes clucking his tongue.

"It is kind of you to consider my welfare, señor. I think

34

you need have no worry. I am an autonomist, yes, but I've never taken any part in politics. It is true that my son Mateo was at one time much wrought-up about the political situation. He was what we call an *exaltado*. It is one of the reasons I sent him to college in New York, to give him a chance to cool off. But I feel sure that the army will not hold this against me."

"All I ask is transportation to Santiago."

"And you shall certainly get it, *señor*. But just now . . ."

"What about just now?"

"The trip, *señor*. It is almost thirty miles, and very rough miles they are. I don't think you would survive it."

"Why, damn it, man, I'm sound as a—"

"Hold still, please!"

The planter leaned forward in his chair and very gently, apologetically, he stretched wide-open George's left eye. Then he opened George's mouth. He sighed.

"*Señor,* I am no physician. But I have lived in Cuba all my life, and I know the symptoms."

"You mean malaria?"

"Worse than that. It is what we call *el vomito negro*. But you know it by the name of another color."

"Good God! You mean I've got—"

"The yellow fever, *señor*."

Everything rocked. He was striving to shout, but couldn't. Collapsing on the flagstones of the terrace, he was suddenly and tumultuously sick. And the stuff *was* black.

He never knew it when they carried him to bed.

CHAPTER VII

DAYS AND NIGHTS checkerboarded, some clear-cut, others fuzzy. The days were worst. Conceivably, he sometimes slept at night, he was uncertain of this, sleep and no-sleep being all but indistinguishable. The daylight, though, hurt his face, especially his eyes. The windows of this bedroom were many and they were large. The persons who shared the room with George, vague ghostly shapes, were careful to keep closed the jalousies; still, the sunlight, though diverted upward, crashed through, to be reflected by a white ceiling. Toss as he would, that light beat down upon George, stinging him. Sometimes he cried out against it and tried to push it away. Always it made his head ache and shredded the ends of his nerves.

Even more painful was his thirst. The shivering had ceased, but he craved water incessantly.

He was aware of those who attended him—when he was aware of them at all—as hands rather than as persons. He seldom saw, but often felt them. They held the glass to his mouth, wiping away spittle and vomit afterward. They mopped his face. They changed the pillow slip.

Sometimes, for a little while, he would be lucid.

He saw a middle-aged stranger with steel-rimmed glasses, who must have been the physician. This man looked worried.

Once he saw Don Diego. The planter, tall, handsome, simply stood at the foot of the bed. George tried to talk to him, to thank him; but the figure faded.

36

Shad-Face the Indian, whose real name unexpectedly turned out to be Wilma, often was at hand. She never said anything. Her expression was one of truculence, or at least intense impatience; yet her hands were marvelously gentle.

Manuelo, too, was sometimes there, usually at night. Manuelo was eager to please, but he was careful not to talk too much; and when he thought that George was asleep, he would sit utterly still for hours.

Those nights were quiet. No sound echoed through the house. The weather was mild, without wind or rain. Only in the night there would be the braying of jackasses, now near at hand, now far away.

"Cuban nightingales, we call them," Manuelo said.

The *Señorita* Ana he saw less often, less distinctly too. She would sit at the side of his bed, her hands folded in her lap like one who listens to a lesson, and regard him with wide eyes. Those eyes, he saw at last, were a very dark, rich brown. In certain lights they showed specks of gold.

Señorita Ana made no attempt to talk to him; and not often did he see or feel her do anything to nurse him, for she left this work to Wilma. The stout Indian always was there when the Señorita Ana was.

"Isn't that carrying the duenna system a bit too far?" was George Heritage's thought. "Hell, who'd be afraid of me, in the shape I'm in now? I couldn't rape a constipated cockroach."

This struck him as very funny, and he chuckled.

Yet the Señorita Ana Pineda was alone, sitting on the edge of her chair, alert, watchful, when at last the fever went away.

Suddenly he could breathe air and see things in focus.

He was far from well. He was pitifully weak. But the cramps in his stomach had gone, as had the burning in his face and loins. Though he remained thirsty, he had no thought of vomiting. He knew who he was and where he was.

He knew who *she* was too. He could have greeted her with a smile, but something told him that it was no time for smiling.

37

"You are very lovely," he whispered.

"You're not delirious any longer."

"Did I say that when I was?"

This was daytime, and the jalousies were tipped up, most of the light coming from above; moreover, she sat with her back to the windows. Yet he could have sworn that he saw her blush.

"You said many things. You called me Lopez and said I was dead and had no right to come back and look at you."

"Oh."

She leaned close, her breath caught up.

"Are you *sure* he's dead?" she whispered.

He wetted his lips, fearful that he might not be able to speak.

"He's dead all right," he said at last.

She began to weep. She did this simply, without sobs, without humping her shoulders, or sniffling.

"So it was your brother?" said George. "I should have known. I . . . I thought you mistook me for a lover, out there."

She shook her head.

"I don't have a lover," she said.

She said it as quietly, as though reporting that she didn't have yellow hair. She was not indignant.

George Heritage had had little experience with women who wept. He had supposed that nine times out of ten it was a trick, that they *turned on* the tears as they might turn a water spigot, intent upon getting their way. But here he faced silent grief, the most terrible sort. There were no hysterics; there was no accusation.

"Lopez? That was the name of a Cuban patriot, wasn't it?"

She nodded weakly.

"I ought to've guessed it the second I saw you. I'd noticed that his initials were cut out of every place you'd look for a monogram. How did you know the *Hina* was coming?"

"He wrote me. I had heard that she was sighted off Purisima Concepcion; don't ask me how. I was expecting him. He would come at night. Our father could not be told that he was being disobeyed. Mateo was going to fight for the cause, but he'd use a different name. That was to protect the property, and father."

"And then *I* came . . . You'd heard the *Hina* was in, but you hadn't heard about the coast guard boat?"

"Not then. I did later. But you had the fever by that time."

"How long have I been this way?"

"Eight days."

She put out a hand and covered one of his.

"You . . . you're sure, *señor?* You actually *saw* it happen?"

"Not actually, no; but the next best thing. I was chained by the side of your brother. I saw them take him out, with three others, and I heard the volley. When I got outside a few minutes later all four of them had been shot."

"They were dead?"

"They were dead all right. Yes."

It was best to be brutal. She appreciated it. She nodded. "Thank you, *señor.*"

"Suppose somebody recognized your brother and told the soldiers who he really was? It was a big crowd. And he must be known around here?"

"I thought of that. It's possible, of course."

"They'd come here then, wouldn't they?"

"Oh, yes. My father thinks that because he has kept out of politics he will be permitted to run a plantation. But it's not so. Mateo was right. There is no neutrality permitted in this war."

Engrossed, they had not heard the horses; but now they heard boots in the hall below, and a tinkle of spurs.

"My dear captain"—it was Don Diego's voice—"while I am delighted to see you, of course, I'm confused. I have already paid the fee for being allowed to cut my cane."

"Oh, to be sure, to be sure!" This was a young voice, cocky. "It's another matter we come here on, sir. Your guest—"

The pause was planned; the two in the sickroom could be sure of it.

Soon, no doubt satisfied by what he had seen in the face of Don Diego, who was hardly a man to lie expertly, they heard:

"General Gomez would speak to this Yanqui."

"He is ill. He has the fever."

"We know. But this is the eighth day. He should either be past the crisis, or else dead."

"You have a search warrant, captain?"

"Do I not carry one at my hip? And each of my men outside there, he carries one too."

A pause, a sigh, then:

"Very well. Come along upstairs."

The planter gave a cry of pleasure when he saw George, and went swiftly to him, and put a hand on his shoulder.

"You survive! Good!"

"Is it?"

The insurgent officer was very young, hardly more than a boy, slim, trim. Clicking his heels, he saluted George.

"You are *Señor* Heritage of Boston, U. S. A.?"

"Guilty."

The captain smiled. It was a brilliant smile, as he knew.

"*Señor*, permit me to congratulate you on your recovery."

"He must have some days yet," Don Diego interposed. "Two, three——"

"Oh, to be sure! But then he will go with us to General Gomez."

"Suppose I don't want to go?" George asked suddenly.

The smile again.

"*Señor*, we have the means with which to persuade you."

"I see."

The captain leaned close, dropping his voice.

"A pity, *señor*. You should have died. It would have been better."

He smiled.

CHAPTER VIII

CAPTAIN CALIXTO BALLETE Y SIERRA, against all probability, as George thought, turned out to be a most interesting and enlightening companion, or captor. He was anything but the popular picture of an outlaw. Flashily handsome, talkative, he was fastidious about his person: his boots glittered gallantly; his sword was silver-hilted; his pistol had a pearl stock; in his white jipijapa hat—George would have called it a Panama—he had thrust, jauntily, the bright blue cockade of the revolution. He had traveled in Europe, had studied at the University of Madrid, and, more important, the moment he ceased to play act proved to be thoughtful, amiable, entertaining. He spoke no English, but his Spanish was not vulgar, and he was tolerant of George's halting speech and patient about repeating things.

The journey took a long day, and it was a trying one. The two privates who trailed this pair—at least, George assumed that they were privates: except for the cockades and Ballete's sword none of the three rebels wore any part of a uniform—were glum, unattractive men. Ballete did all the talking.

"Lopez I can understand, captain, from what I've read. But your Ten Years War! Where was the purpose of that? It was destructive, all tear-down, all burn-up, and to what end? It never did spread over the whole island. It was stuck right here in Oriente Province."

"Ah, *señor,* we were hoodwinked."

"You mean Spain sold you down the river?"

"Eh? I do not know what that means. But Spain—yes, and all the Peninsulars who work here in Cuba until they can make enough money to go back home—they were weary of fighting, and they promised us the moon. And we, poor fools, we signed a treaty and gave up our arms. And what happened? Where were those reforms? Taxes went even further up. We were granted representation in the Cortes, oh, yes: *three* out of four hundred and thirty! The Captain-General became the Governor-General; and what difference did that make? He was still a czar from Spain. The royal decrees were not issued any more, but 'authorizations' were. Just the names changed, that's all. The commercial monopoly became the coasting trade. The right to banishment became the law of vagrancy. Words! We have no more liberty than before, and we'll never get any unless we fight for it."

"You call this fighting—burning cane fields?"

"*Señor*, believe me, it is the only method that will win. Unless some power helps us, like your own U. S. A., *señor*, how can we ever expect to prevail against Spain? Spain is very much larger than Cuba. And richer. And more populous. Spain is a touchy nation, you understand, *señor*! She's proud! With all the world watching her, she would never consent to make a bargain with us. I tell you, the only way we can get our liberty is by making ourselves so expensive that Madrid will drop us like a hot poker."

They were treading a narrow path, all the while going up, beside a wood of *corojo* palms and royal *piñon*.

"Wasn't that what Cuba tried at the time of the Ten Years War? And what did it get you then?"

"At least it taught us never to trust Madrid again."

"But it ruined the country!"

"So?"

"Wouldn't you call that cutting off the nose to spite the face? Cutting off the whole head, for that matter?"

"Perhaps. But what good is it to have a head if you can only hang it? But you look tired, *señor*. Shall we rest a while?"

One of the soldiers went back down the trail to act as sentry. The other picked bananas. They were very small bananas, the best George had ever tasted. Captain Ballete produced a chunk of cheese and a horn of acceptable, if somewhat sweet, wine. It was good to lie there in the shade, looking out over this lush polychromatic land. It was so quiet and peaceful . . .

When Ballete waked him it was with a whispered apology. Unless they kept going, he explained, they might be benighted.

Soon afterward they were challenged.

"*Quien va?*"

They could see nobody. The two privates and George came to an immediate, prudent stop, but Ballete, pushing back his jipijap hat so that it hung by the cord around his neck, rode forward.

"*Cuba libre!*"

Three men emerged from behind trees. Two had rifles, old rifles, George noted—single-shots. Each had a machete. They saluted Ballete and talked with him for a little while; then they stood aside to let the party pass.

This happened again a few miles further, and George commented upon the challenge, which was the same.

"You are observant, *señor*. Yes, the Creoles do cry '*Quien va?*' just as they greet one another with their hats pushed back. And the Peninsulars keep their hats on and call '*Quien vivre?*' but we mustn't count on this. The dirty *guerrilleros* will sometimes uncover and cry '*Quien va?*' just to get you to come close."

The Spanish army, heavily reinforced, and with more reinforcements on the way, and the rebel army, hidden in the hills, were not the only groups of military men in Cuba, George was told. There was in addition a sort of militia, men mostly of Spanish birth—for the Cubans themselves had not been permitted to train as soldiers—all over the island. They were largely officials of one sort or another, virtually all government workers being Spaniards from Spain. When they were Cubans, as some recent recruits were, they were Cubans of the most criminal type. These were what Ballete called *guerrilleros,* and it was obvious from the way he said it that he hated them even more fervently than he hated the Spanish soldiers themselves.

"There is yet another armed rider, *señor,* and he too goes in gangs. We call them the *plateados.* They are robbers, rapists. They lurk in places of little population and attack when the real men are away at war. They steal, they burn. A *plateado* is the lowest of the low. I shall point out one when we get around this curve ahead. But this scoundrel isn't really low—now."

Such grisley humor did not go down well with George Heritage, who, however, said nothing. The sight, around the bend, was a gruesome one. What had been a man, hanging by the neck from the limb of a large *ceiba,* was surrounded by buzzards, the beaks of which were sopped with his guts and blood. The buzzards flumped off a short distance with cries of annoyance when the party approached. Little was left but the clothes, the bones, and the stink.

"We call that the Tree of Justice. We used a tree in the camp itself, at first; but that became too, well, fragrant."

Yet this same young man, when camp was reached, was solicitous about George's condition. He found a tent, a cot, meat, bread and some rum. Having touched none of these, he went off to report.

Eating, drowsy, dog-tired, George surveyed the scene. Nobody seemed interested in him, though such men as did go by smiled. It was sundown, and fires were being lighted. George could not estimate the size of this army, for it was tucked away in little groves and gullies, here and there. There was not much noise, and everybody seemed to go about his own business.

There were no flags, no uniforms, and by no means were all of the men armed with guns, though each had at least a machete. About one in four was a Negro. There were many women, a fact that astonished George. Perhaps a sixth of those within his sight were women, who were as busy

44

as the men, taking in laundry, restringing hammocks, preparing food. George even saw a few children.

There were not many tents like the one he was in, and what there were were not arranged in any recognizable order. There were, however, hammocks, hundreds of them, strung between trees.

The ground was trampled, but it was not slovenly. There were no broken bottles, fish heads or bits of bone. Latrines were at some distance from the sleeping and eating places.

Somewhere to George's left, somebody strummed a guitar, humming absent-mindedly. To the right there was a chorus:

> *Al com-bat-te corred batame-ses; o!*
> *Que la patria os compempla or-gulla-spa —*

It was no scene of hilarity, but it was . . . *homey.*

Odd. And these were bandits.

It was dark. Ballete was shaking him very gently.

"Uh?"

The camp was quiet, the fires low. Now and then some sentry or officer on rounds cried *"Alerta!"* and got his response. Otherwise there was only a tinny rustle of banana fronds—that and snoring.

"The general has said he will not receive you now. I made it plain that you were tired."

"Gracias. The general works at night, then?"

"The general works all the time. He will see you at four o'clock."

"God. But what for? You never have told me that."

"Señor, it is not for me to know. I am only a staff officer, but I believe that you will find the talk interesting. And now, sweet dreams, *señor. Buenas noches."*

"Buenas noches."

45

MAXIMO GOMEZ must have been in his seventies, and he had never laughed. His eyes were the color of oiled steel. His dead-white mustachios drooped. He was smallish, with a girl's waist and a girl's hands. Naturally rigid, a ramrod, he tried to unbend to George, and actually rose when George entered the tent. He extended a hand. The grip was firm, meaning to be friendly; but the hand itself was as cold as his eyes.

"You are the one who survived. Congratulations, sir."

"Thank you."

"You have had your chocolate?"

"I'm afraid not."

"But—" Seated again, he waggled his hands, unable to understand. After all, it was nearly dawn. "Well, you must have some."

"Yes."

With a small scowl, Gomez sent away Ballete, the conducting officer. Then he picked up a Colt .44 revolver, holding it by the barrel, and rapped the butt upon the table. A soldier appeared.

"Chocolate. For him."

There were a dozen folding stools with canvas seats, and there was a large table, nothing more. On the table, near the pistol, were a leather case scrammed with dispatches and a pile of U. S. newspapers. The papers, George noted, were from New York. He recognized those rabid rivals, the *World* and the *Journal*, there were also copies of the *Herald*, the *Sun*, the *Times*, the *Tribune*, the *Evening Post* and the *Journal of Commerce*.

Gomez folded his hands, though he did not relax.

"You must tell me about it."

He had a reedy voice. It might have come from an unpleasant old woman.

"Of course."

George had expected this. Gomez would have had spies at Purisima Concepcion, and so he would know what had happened just outside of the prison on that memorable morning less than two weeks ago. How he had traced George to the Pineda plantation was another matter. But the man was a hill fighter, a hit-and-run expert, and he would have had all sorts of contacts among country people. The massacre at Purisima must have loomed large even in the bloody annals of Cuba, while the single escape surely had been sensational. It was no more than human—though the truth is the man didn't *look* human—for the commander-in-chief to wish to hear the story at first hand.

George told the tale simply. The insurrectionist chief was all attention. Not once did he shift or blink those icy gray eyes.

This time there were no congratulations. The general just stared at George in silence for a little while, then asked; "You did not, then, sign up in the Army of Cuba?"

"No, sir. I believed I had taken a civilian job."

"And so you are not, theoretically, one of my men?"

"Why, of course not."

"*Señor* Heritage, if the *Hina* had not been overtaken; if you'd landed those guns and that dynamite and found you were expected to serve in a revolutionary army, what would you have done?"

"I don't know. I haven't had much time to think about that. I might have written it off as experience and gone home. Or I might have taken the job anyway, if the pay was right."

47

"We of the Army of Cuba do not get pay, only glory."

"That might be enough for you but it wouldn't be for me."

"I see. And what do you propose to do now?"

"Get to Santiago, to the U. S. consul."

"Señor Heritage, you must realize that if you went back to your native country telling a story of how you were tricked into sailing for Cuba, it would not look well for the Cuban cause. We raise most of our funds in the United States."

George only shrugged. He was trying to read the newspapers upside-down.

"Well, I'd tell the truth, if I were asked."

"You'd *be* asked!"

He said this with such vehemence that George started, glancing up. But again George shrugged.

"All I can say is that maybe the cause had better be a little more careful in picking its enlistment agents. Say, could I look at some of those newspapers? I don't come from New York myself, but . . ."

"I'm coming to those."

Gomez put a hand on the pile. It was a small hand, waxy, pale, and so thin that you could almost read the type through it; yet somehow it contrived to suggest a claw.

"First you must know that these papers only came in a few hours ago. They were smuggled from Key West into what we call a *balsa*— that means a bag—a small, landlocked harbor. They contain the accounts of the mass execution at Purisima Concepcion."

"So soon?"

"The colonel in charge at Purisima sent his report by telegraph to Havana, but he neglected to mention your escape. It would have made him look silly. He simply reported that all sixteen men had been executed. It was neater that way."

"More military."

"We have men in headquarters at Havana, some of them close to Campos himself. A copy of this report was made,

48

and it was sent by fast boat to Tampa. Our friends there tele-
graphed it to the junta in New York, who gave it to the
newspapers; but Tampa, where they knew something about
you, had added a detail. Wisely: They had pointed out that
you were a bona fide, native-born U. S. citizen."

"Quite right."

"They didn't have to make a martyr out of you. The
newspapers could be counted upon to do that. Here! And
excuse me."

George couldn't believe it at first. Thinking that he must
be the victim of some tasteless hoax, he looked up. General
Gomez was taking dispatches out of the leather case. Outside,
the camp was just getting up: children were crying; women
were gossiping; the men were making fires.

George looked again at the papers. He had never seen his
name in print so many times—and such large print, too.

Except for the masthead, the weather, and a slogan in the
left ear, Pulitzer's paper, the *World,* had given him its entire
front page, as had the *Journal,* Hearst's. The others were almost as bad, even the arch-conservative *Post.*

UNCLE SAM, WHO TIED YOUR HANDS?

AVENGE HERITAGE!

HOW MUCH LONGER WILL WE STAND FOR THIS?

SHOT IN THE BACK

The other filibusters and sailors were mentioned, but
George was the feature of every story.

"Well, I'll be a sonofagun!"

"Eh?"

The general looked up.

"Nothing."

Fascinated, George read on. Or else he simply stared—for
there were pictures too. No photograph ever had been taken
of George, but this hadn't deterred the newspaper editors,
always a notably ingenious lot. An "artist's conception" of
the scene behind that Cuban prison appeared in most of the
papers. In each case the artist, who clearly never had been
south of State Island, penciled in a large number of palm

49

trees as local color—usually date palms, which don't grow in Cuba. In each case, too, he placed a glorified George Heritage in the foreground in some heroic pose, head high, arms widespread.

The facts, such as they were, had not been distorted, only puffed. Given that official report—which was virtually all that they *had* been given—the editors had done very well indeed. George was in business for himself in Boston, a recently set-up business, without immediate associates, and he had been on the road much of the time. He had no close relations, not many friends. He had worked his way through Bowdoin, where he had not been active in either social life or sports; that is to say, information about him, and especially information of the intimate sort the papers wanted, had been hard to get. But the papers had done their best. They had even dug up remote cousins George himself had forgotten. From the massed descriptions of George supplied by these relatives, some of whom hadn't seen him since he was nine or ten years old, one of the papers had assembled a "composite portrait." It looked like Lord Byron.

"You are, *señor*, what the French would call a *'cause célèbre.'* "

"By golly, it looks like it!"

The general had put the dispatches aside.

. "You should feel pleased that all unwittingly you have struck such a blow for Cuba."

"Oh, I do."

"Contributions will double. There will be resolutions, editorials. Perhaps eventually there will be so much pressure brought to bear on Washington that our army will be recognized. That's what we need more than anything else."

"Yes . . ." George looked down at the papers. "Makes me think of where Tom Sawyer and Huck Finn are thought to have been drowned and they come back to their own funeral. They hide in the organ loft of the church and watch it. A very funny scene."

"It must be."

George chuckled.

"All the same, it's going to make them look mighty foolish when I come back."

"Is it?"

George looked up, not liking the tone of that voice.

"Well, you certainly haven't any right to keep me here."

"If you return to the States it would ruin this story, so beautiful . . . even if it's not true. It would make everybody concerned look silly. It would deprive us of a thing we need most of all just now—a martyr. If you return, it would be the worst thing that ever happened to our cause."

"*If* I return?"

"But, no. We are not going to keep you here. This is a mobile camp, and the saints alone know where it will be next week. And you might find those who pitied you here, for after all you did a very dashing thing. They might help you to escape."

"All right, so what in hell *are* you going to do with me?"

The general folded his hands on the table before him and turned those terrible gray eyes full upon George.

"It pains me to tell you this, *senor*, but we are going to shoot you."

CHAPTER X

Mateo Pineda, alias Lopez, had been the youngest of those returning, doomed patriots aboard the *Hina;* but all had been young. The first officer of the Army of Cuba George had been privileged to meet, Calixto Ballete y Sierra, was not out of his teens. George had noted in camp, too, the prevailing air of youth.

There were exceptions, the most prominent being Gomez himself. Yet at the council Gomez had called to ratify his decision to have George executed, only one other man could have been over thirty.

That one was alone in other respects. Since he occupied the far end of the table from Gomez, it might have been taken to mean that he was second in command. He was a mulatto; the rest were white.

From what Geroge had seen of the people of Cuba they were, while not midgets, on the whole somewhat slighter and shorter than the people of Maine. It was not to be expected that many of the soldiers in that mountain camp would be plump. The life hardly was conducive to obesity. Yet, if not frail—for they all looked wiry, even the aged Gomez— they were generally, slim, small of bone.

Once again the mulatto at the far end of the table was an exception. He loomed enormous. He must have stood six-three and weighed 225 pounds, yet there wasn't a super-fluous ounce of flesh on him. His skin was like burnished copper. His beard was exquisitely oiled and tapered. Though he did not clank with ornaments, sartorially he outshone even Ballete. Most of the others smelled of sleep, of saddle leather, or even, at this early hour, of sweat; but the big mulatto smelled of perfume—a very expensive French perfume.

It was at this man that George looked when he spoke, for he had been told that court lawyers concentrate upon one member of a jury.

He made himself heard. A rapist, a deserter, a *plateado* might be hanged out of hand; but George Heritage was something else. As the sole survivor of Purisima Concepcion, he was a hero here in camp. Officially dead, in truth he was very much alive, as these men could see. The colonels and the majors—Ballete was the only officer present under the rank of major—regarded him with undisguished admiration. It isn't every day that you meet a myth.

"You knew about this?" George whispered.

"I suspected it, I didn't know for certain," Ballete whispered back. "But what would you have me do, *señor?* If I told you of my expectance it might spoil your sleep."

Glowering, pushing the dispatch case aside, the general set forth the reasons for his decision. He hated to have to justify himself.

"No matter how this man came to our land, no matter how little good will for our cause he had, this remains: he *did* come here! He was captured. He lost his explosives, and all but lost his life. I'll not deny that his escape called for quick thinking, for courage, and speed. Death is a bitter reward for such a feat. Yet death, gentlemen, is what we deal in here. We can face nothing else."

He tapped the newspapers.

"You've had these translated. You must know, even if you know nothing else about the Yankees, that the chorus will swell . . . and swell . . . It is the greatest thing that has happened to the Cuban cause. Now we can look for funds and for supplies—even recognition."

53

He was angry, for he sensed opposition.

"On the other hand, if we turn this man back to the U. S. A., we'd make fools of ourselves. The 'martyr' would evaporate. The stock of the Republic of Cuba would fall. A feeling of embarrassment would have set in. Yankees would prefer to forget this land. And if we're forgotten, gentlemen, we are lost."

The camp stirred. Eggs spluttered in a pan. Somebody cursed.

"You may ask why I don't adopt some less severe measure for keeping Señor Heritage out of sight? I'll tell you. If I were Campos in Havana, if the situation were reversed, then my course would be clear. I'd throw the prisoner into the deepest dungeon of Morro Castle, and if anybody asked about him I'd deny that I had ever even heard of him. Then, when the war was over, I'd let him out, shake his hand, give him a cigar, and apologize for the inconvenience I'd caused."

He pounded the table.

"But we haven't got a Morro Castle. We can't keep this man forever bound. He had already demonstrated his ability to escape from tighter bonds than we can afford to fasten upon him. And even if he didn't wish to go away, he could become lost, or cut off and captured. If word of his existence leaked out he could be kidnapped from us. Why not? Stranger things have happened.

"No, gentlemen, this prisoner must be dead. Not merely dead on paper but *actually* dead. Here's the warrant. I could sign it alone, but I thought that in a matter so serious you would wish to express yourselves as being in accord with your commander-in-chief."

Nobody reached out to touch the paper, though neither did anyone shrink from it. George regarded it dispassionately.

"Well, gentlemen?"

Still nobody stirred.

"I think," said the mulatto at the end of the table, "that we should hear what the prisoner has to say for himself."

54

Gomez was furious. A vein in his temple throbbed.

"That is, of course, customary," he conceded. "I had thought to dispense with it here, in the interest of time. But if the others . . ."

He looked around. He got no answer. He nodded curtly to George.

"Do you have anything to say, sir?"

"I sure do," said George; and he rose.

General Gomez had spoken with feeling, but he'd remained seated. That was a mistake. A Boston politician once had told George that any speaker who wished to put over his point should get up on something, "even if it's only his own feet." He should be *above* his audience. In no circumstances, this man had said, should he remain seated. "Nobody can really stretch his lungs and warm his ass at the same time," he had said. George remembered this. So he got up.

"Thank you," he said gravely.

He did not plead, for that, too, he believed, would have been a tactical error. He demanded.

He had a more receptive audience here than he'd had on the previous occasion of the court-martial. These Cubans were younger, more liberal. They had, too, more English than the others; and they were closer, physically and culturally, to the Yankee of the mainland. Moreover, George's own Spanish, in the course of his convalescence, had increased. His vocabulary, if limited, was forthright. It was a soldier's vocabulary, thanks to the tutelage of Manuelo.

He told these outlaws that if they murdered him, the whole world would spit upon them. They might think that they could conceal such a crime, he cried, but it would come out. He'd rise from his very grave to haunt them. And the majestic United States of America, when *it* learned of that shameful assassination, that stab in the back, would *it* smile upon a cause headed by the men who had done it? He could damn' well assure them that it wouldn't.

He pounded the table, as Gomez had done.

Then he changed his tone. He spread his hands. After all, he reminded these men, he was a demolition expert, something you don't find behind every cactus. Leaving aside their hopes of Heaven, where was their common sense? Did they want to win this war or did they simply want to sit around like a parcel of students spouting big words about military necessity?

He laughed, a laugh choked with contempt. He sat down.

For some time, again, there was silence. The men stared at the death warrant as though entoiled, as though they expected *it* to say something. Only the mulatto at one end of the table and the commander-in-chief at the other, regarded George Heritage.

Gomez fairly trembled, and the vein in his temple seemed about to burst. George feared, for a moment there, that the little general would snatch the revolver from the table and shoot him dead. They were only about five feet apart.

The mulatto broke the silence, his voice a resonant baritone.

"General, the dispatch boat that brought these papers also brought us six hundred pounds of dynamite, isn't that so?"

Gomez only nodded, possibly not trusting himself to speak.

"We could use dynamite. Surely, general, we are all agreed that this revolt must not be allowed to get stalled here in Oriente, as the others have. And you have given me the honor of leading that break-out for the west, yes?"

Gomez nodded, watching him.

"Dynamite could be telling in such a thrust, general. This man has already had the fever and is immune—an important point. And he is right: we don't find blasters behind every bush."

"But if—"

"General, our whole cause hangs upon my success in breaking into Pinar del Rio, so that we can claim that the movement is nationwide. And you promised me a free hand."

He put his elbows on the table, leaning forward. He picked up the death warrant and read it swiftly. A secretary appeared from nowhere, put down a pen and a bottle of ink, then vanished.

Gomez said slowly, "General Maceo, do I take it that you refuse to sign that paper?"

"Certainly not, sir."

He smiled, and signed it. He passed it to the man on his left, who signed it and passed it along. It went around the table. Even Ballete y Sierra signed it. And in this way, it came back to the mulatto, who blotted it, folded it, and put it into his purse.

"Let us say, then, that this court has condemned the prisoner to death. And that it has appointed me his executioner. Pending certain tasks I have in mind in connection with the break-out to the west, I shall suspend this execution temporarily—provided, of course, that I get the service I need. Is it understood?"

Gomez studied their faces, all of them. He drew a long wobbly breath. He scowled.

"Dismissed," he muttered.

Lieutenant General Antonio Maceo rose, reaching for his hat. He crooked a finger at George Heritage.

"You," he said. "Come with me, please."

CHAPTER XI

Four days later George and Ballete, with an escort of
six men, started for the Pineda plantation. Near noon they
stopped to rest their horses and to eat.

Though strength seeped back into George, he still was
weak. He tired easily; and now, like an old man, he was
glad of a chance to sit, his back against a tree, and sleepily
survey the plain below.

He was not unhappy. His physical condition was at least
as good as could be expected. True, his position in camp
had not been regularized, and nobody seemed to know
whether he was a prisoner or a staff officer; but at the moment this didn't matter. Though the rains would soon start,
presently the weather was perfect. The prospect of calling
again upon Don Diego, and upon his daughter, was a pleas-
ant one.

The ground sloped away sharply at this point. Just below
George, so close that he could almost have kicked it, was
the top of an enormous silk-cotton tree, as fussily tremulous
as was the clump of bamboo slightly farther down. Still,
farther down on the floor of the plain, was a field of cut
cane, part of the Pineda holding. Sunlight soaked everything.
George yawned.

"A pomegranate, *señor?*"

"Thank you."

A wonderful land, he reflected, where you could eat

pomegranates as casually as in Maine you might eat apples.

". . . is what we call it," Ballete was saying, seemingly in answer to some drowsy question put by George. "We say a thing like Purisima is written in the Book of Blood. There have been many entries in that book. And there'll be others."

It startled George. Blood! In this place of rainbow colors it was but to be expected, he supposed, that blood should play a part. Yet, must the whole countryside be drenched in it?

What he had found in the camp in the mountains, as at Purisima Concepcion, was ordered ferocity. The Cubans could and often did laugh right up from out of their guts; but they went on training themselves for slaughter as they did so. Even while they sang, they were honing their machetes. The most persistent sound in the camp, heard at all hours of the day and often far into the night, was that ominous, unceasing slish-slish of steel on stone.

He shook himself. He must think of something else.

"The Book of Blood, eh?"

"*Si, señor.* Another pomegranate? A shell of wine?"

"Thanks."

The peremptory manner in which Antonio Maceo had ordered George to follow him no doubt was assumed only for effect in front of the commander-in-chief. In his own tent, as he went about the business of preparing for a bath, the second-in-command had been kindness itself. He had asked to hear the story of the escape, and had listened closely, while an orderly filled a washtub with warm water and brought soap, a sponge and a sleazy towel.

Maceo undressed himself. Here was an heroic figure. Muscles that were lithe, not bunchy, rippled underneath a light-brown satin skin as the man stepped into a hip-tub and started to splash. But Maceo didn't sing, for he was busy listening to George. Just as there was not a weakness in that magnificent physique, no soft spot, so there was not in his manner as he washed the slightest hint of self-consciousness. Standing there naked, thoughtfully scrubbing, he was as naive as a god of classical days.

"This urine, it was dark yellow or light?"

"Very light, sir. I had no control over that."

"Of course. Now, is nitroglycerine yellow?"

"It can be. Or it can be slightly grayish. Or clear. It doesn't bead, like urine."

"Even if you shake it?"

"General, you *don't* shake it."

"I see."

"It has a somewhat oily sheen."

"In other words, the liquid you flourished on that occasion, *señor*, didn't look like nitroglycerine at all?"

"They didn't know that," George pointed out.

Maceo rinsed himself and started to towel his gleaming, bronze-hard body. But he continued to ask questions, and soon he had George defining and describing nitro-cellulose, cordite, tonite, ammonite, trinitrotoluene, and nitroglycerine itself, which George said should properly be called glyceryl trinitrate.

"Good," said Maceo. "Have you had breakfast?"

"Why, I ate at General Gomez's."

"Then you haven't had breakfast. A dry biscuit and half a cup of chocolate, eh?"

"Well . . ."

"General Gomez has many estimable qualities, but an appetite is not one of them. He feeds you like a canary. Join me, please."

He ate earnestly but well, not talking except to make certain polite offers. The food was hot, and it was abundant. Afterward the table was cleared, and Maceo's aides came in. George witnessed that conference, though he took no part in it. He had been introduced to each of the members of the staff. Since he had no military rank, they called him, simply, *"señor."* Most of them were white. All of them were gracious. Maceo however gave them no chance to parade their social attainments. He plunged into the business of organizing an invasion of western Cuba.

Afterward, when they had been dismissed, he signaled to George to stay, and gave him a fine cigar.

"You have met my official family. How you are treated depends, of course, upon how valuable you prove yourself to be. You'll work under primitive conditions, and we will make allowances for this. I only wish to remind you that I have made myself responsible for you; and I'm a man who respects his responsibilities. You must not leave camp without my permission. You understand?"

"Perfectly."

"You must not forget, *señor*," he pressed the wallet in his breast pocket—"what I have here."

"I am not likely to forget it."

"Good. Now let's have a look at that dynamite."

It was poor stuff, probably containing no more than thirty percent of nitroglycerine. There was six hundred pounds of it, packed into one large crate. The sticks, each the standard eight inches long, one and a quarter inches in diameter, were wrapped in heavy red paper that bore the name of a California firm. It would sell wholesale in the States for about fifty cents a pound. The paper, George noted, was machine-crimped, not hand-crimped. There were six folds.

George unwrapped a stick, sniffed it, touched it with his tongue, thumbnailed some loose and mortared this into the hollow of his left hand, using the heel of his right hand as a pestle. He put it on a board and got a branch from a fire. He burned the stuff, squatting beside it, studying the brisk, blue-purple flame.

There was a squeal of fright, and he looked up to find himself almost alone. General Maceo, however, remained.

"How does it look, *señor?*"

"I've seen better. But it might do. The bottom of that crate"—he pointed—"looks as if it could have got wet."

"Would that make any difference in the dynamite?"

"It might make it more dangerous to handle. It might

even make the crate itself dangerous. I ought to know when that happened, and whether it was salt water or fresh water, and whether it was just a passing wave or whether the stuff actually soaked in it."

"It shall be done immediately," and he summoned an aide.

"Could you perhaps set off a stick for me now?" Maceo asked a little later.

"How?"

"Why, there are blasting caps right there."

"Yes. Number sixes and number eights. But how are you going to set one of *them* off? By hitting it with a hammer?"

"Oh."

"There are two ways of doing it. One is with an electric box. I could rig that if I had a battery and some wire. Any in camp?"

"I'm afraid not."

"The other way is with safety fuse. And there isn't an inch of that here. I guess somebody just plumb forgot to put it in."

"Wouldn't ordinary cord—?"

"No. Safety's made for the work. It's jute, wrapped in a certain way, and it has a core of granulated black gunpowder. You can time it. If you don't know how long your fuse will take you'd better just stay away from dynamite, that's all."

"And there isn't any other way?"

"Well, you might blaze away with a rifle. A good clean hit in the center of the cap ought to do it. But you'd have to be a marksman!"

"No, no! We can't spare the cartridges. Our men go into battle with only four or five rounds apiece, while the Spaniards carry a hundred and fifty. No. Couldn't you find something here that would serve as safety fuse?"

"I could try."

That search was fruitless, though it had lasted four days. It was then that George got permission from General Maceo to go down to the plain. He had pointed out that it was conceivable that something like safety fuse might be found

62

in the Pineda house or might be obtained through the good offices of Don Diego. Maceo had agreed, stipulating only that George be accompanied by an officer acceptable to him, Maceo, and also by a squad of men who might do a little foraging on the way. George had asked for Captain Balette, and Maceo instantly granted this, arranging to have Balette transferred from Gomez's staff to his own— a transfer Balette himself had been trying for weeks to arrange.

Now Balette put a hand on George's shoulder.

"Shall we be getting on? Have you had enough rest?"

"Sure." He looked curiously at his companion. "You seem eager to get there, captain? Is that to see Don Diego?"

"It is always an honor to meet *Señor* Pineda. But to meet his daughter . . . Ah, that's heaven!"

"Umm. You known her long?"

"Only a few months. I would have to get my parents' permission, of course, before I spoke to her father. And that's not possible right now. But one can hope, can't one?"

"Why, yes, sure. Sure, one can always hope."

A few hours later they came to the lane that led up to the Pineda house.

There was something wrong with that house. Though sunshine remained, the windows were dull, lusterless. No smoke rose from the cooking kiosk, but there was a pall of heavy, dark gray smoke over the farm buildings and the mill. The front door stood open. Buzzards were coming in from the hills.

"I don't like this. Something's happened."

"Come on," said George.

Side by side, they galloped up the lane.

CHAPTER XII

BEES BUZZED in the hibiscus bushes on either side of the door. A hummingbird poked one of the fat scarlet blossoms.

On the threshold lay a linen scarf of the sort that many Cubans wore knotted around their necks. Once white, it was dirty now. It had about it an air of haste, as though somebody having recently dropped it, had been in too much of a hurry to stop and pick it up. George *did* pick it up. The two ends below the place where the knot had been, the ends that would have hung down the wearer's chest, were covered with small, dark brown spots. Those spots might have been red a little while ago.

George looked at Ballete, who looked at him.

They stood on the threshold, almost afraid to go in.

At last George reached out and hammered on the door. "Is anyone home?" he called.

The Pineda house was not large, but as became a structure in a tropical clime it had high ceilings and wide doorways. Though the furniture was in excellent taste, there was not much of it. To George, accustomed to horsehair, heavy drapes, and wall-to-wall carpeting, the house was bare. His voice raised an abundance of echoes.

Out of those echoes came another sound. It was a terrible sound to listen to, eerie and faint.

A man in there was weeping.

They shouted but were not answered. But the weeping

went on. Scarcely heard, yet unmistakable, it overhung them like a cloud as they went from room to room . . . always finding each room empty.

It was on the second floor, in a clothes closet, that at last they came upon Manuelo. He was seated on the floor, rocking back and forth in a paroxysm of grief. When the door opened he shrank from it, covering his head with his arms.

"No, no! Don't hit me again!"

"Where is the señorita?"

George knocked the arms aside, and they saw Manuelo's face.

One eye was closed by purple swelling. The mouth showed a great protuberant blob of crusty, dry blood.

"I tried to stop them. I did all I could."

"Where is she?"

"The *señorita* was not here. She went to Purisima in borrowed clothes, as a peasant, to visit the grave of her brother, may the saints preserve his soul. Wilma was with her."

"And Don Diego?"

"Oh, my God!"

"Was it about me?" George cried.

"No. It was about poor Mateo. Somebody had recognized him, at Purisima just before they shot him."

"Guerrilleros?" asked Ballete.

Manuelo nodded, as they helped him to his feet.

"It was the first my poor master knew of it. He thought his son was in New York. Ah, *Madre Maria.* How he loved that lad! And they said they'd teach him what he should have done to Mateo to keep him from becoming a traitor. I tried to stop them but . . ."

"Where is he?"

"On the terrace."

At least they beat the buzzards there. The terrace by the side of the Pineda house was roofed by a grill over which climbed an enormous bougainvillea. Vine and grill alike had baffled the great, ungainly birds. They hovered just

65

above the lovely purple flowers as they sought an entrance to the terrace below, bumping their beaks, flopping their huge wings.

"Go away, you ghouls!" shrieked Balette, and he fired his revolver at them.

They rose, squawking plaintively. They flumped away, but not far. They settled upon the ground about two hundred feet off, and stood there with high-hunched shoulders, waiting.

There was a great deal of blood. It was splattered in all directions from the figure in the middle of the terrace. This was the work of maniacs. Not a stone was left unspotted.

Don Diego, naked, had been tied, wrists and ankles, face-down, to a ladder. The welts and open cuts were everywhere upon his frail, bony body. He looked less like a man than like a putrefying piece of beef. The flies were having a holiday.

"La muerte a la escalera — the death on the ladder," Ballete whispered. "They do it with bullwhips."

He knelt, in blood, on one side of Don Diego, while George Heritage knelt on the other. There was nothing that they could do. It needed no physician to attest that this man was dead.

He had died while still in the first shock of having learned that his son had disobeyed him, and had been shot. They could only hope that the shock had numbed him, so that he had hardly felt the pain.

Ballete got the other knee down, and he clasped his hands under his chin, bowing his head, closing his eyes. George, embarrassed as he always was when somebody prayed in his presence, rose.

When Ballette rose, a moment later, he was openly, shamelessly weeping. Yet his voice was even.

"We must do what we can for him. We must bury him, at least."

"I'll get Manuelo. And a shovel."

They were trying not to look at the thing at their feet, so hideously cut, so pulped and slashed, so torn to shreds. Ballete glared at the buzzards, who waited in a ragged row.

"It's another chapter in that book I told you about, *señor*."

"Aye," said George. "The Book of Blood."

CHAPTER XIII

"MY THREE BEST ALLIES," General Gomez was wont to say, "are June, July, and August."

George was soon to see what he meant. When the rains came they came abruptly, furiously. Everything stuck. Clothing grew moldy and green. The clatter on palm fronds and tents was so loud that even the simplest order had to be shouted. Now and then, with that same fiendish abruptness the rain would cease. Men's ears would ring in the sudden silence. Mist rose from the ground, blotting the puddles from sight. It writhed as though in pain, grayish-white. It broke away from moving things, baffled, but immediately closed in behind them. The sun might come out for a little while; but always the rain returned. They could hear it marching across the hills: a thin, tinny sound from the distance, as the foliage was shredded, but it grew louder and louder until it was like a clang of gongs. The campers could count upon it. They could time it. They knew just when to take cover.

With the rain came fever. There were two large hospitals in camp, buildings made of *piñon* trunks plastered together with mud, upholding corrugated iron roofs. There were several excellent physicians, though there were no nurses. There was a shortage of cots, but the hospitals were floored so that patients at least could be kept off the night earth, which "sweated" even in the dry season.

There were many kinds of fever. The commonest was malaria, which came and went intermittently but was at its worst during the rains. Yellowjack was rare. The outlook of Cubans upon this scourge amazed George Heritage: they took it for granted, regarding it as lightly as mumps and measles were regarded in the States. You got it, you suffered; if you died, too bad! If you lived, you'd never get *el vomito pieto* again; for unlike malaria it was not recurrent. It was better, then, if you had already had it. When he was putting in for George's services, one of the first things General Maceo mentioned in his favor was that he was now immune to yellowjack.

Sometimes indeed the Cubans seemed almost affectionate toward *el vomito negro*, which struck their enemies more viciously than it struck them. The "friendly fever" George once heard it called. For there was no immunity among the soldiers sent from Spain, who, untoughened by the tropics, succumbed in droves. No Spanish officer could know, in the morning, what proportion of last night's men he could count upon. This was what Gomez meant when he called June, July, and August his most powerful allies.

Not only was the air of the camp different, but so were the sounds. Meals were now furtive, huddled, cold. There was no chance to hang wash, very little chance even for gossip.

Yet the spirit of these men was by no means swept away. Fatalists, they took it with a shrug. They were unfailingly polite. They would squat in their makeshift, doorless huts and flash toothy smiles at George as he passed. Hunkered under the overhang of a cliff, drenched in spray, inches from an almost solid sheet of rain, they would wave. Even the sentries, miserable, exposed, still sang out, "Buenas dias."

Tents, like tarpaulins, were at a premium. George Heritage and young Captain Ballete, having both, were looked upon as millionaires. Their tent was one Ballete had requisitioned for his prisoner. The tarpaulin had been issued to George as a cover for the dynamite.

In addition, they had an orderly. Stumpy Manuelo had no wish to remain alone at the plantation, chancing a return of the *guerrilleros*. Field hands and house servants alike had fled, for the mill had been wrecked, the storehouse burned, the house itself stripped of everything valuable. An exception was Wilma, who was with the *Señorita* Ana and would stay with her. Manuelo was afraid of Wilma, whom he greatly admired. Nor did he worry about the *Señorita* Ana, as did both of the men he waited upon. To George, as to Ballete, it seemed a horrid thing that so young and tender a female should thus be thrust into a world at war, with no other attendant than a surly middle-aged Indian. Ana had just lost her brother, then her father, her home too. In these circumstances would she keep her reason? Wouldn't she be likely to do something reckless? Manuelo, who after all did know her better than either of the others, did not think so. He shook his head. "The *señorita* was no fool," he said. And she had Wilma with her. What better protection?

Somehow, he would never say how, Manuelo had sent word to Shad-Face at Purisima, warning her and the *señorita* to go to Santiago, where the *señorita* had relatives, and, if possible, to go even farther away for the rest of the war; he had suggested Havana. Manuelo had not the slightest tremor of doubt that the two women had done this.

Manuelo was, at bottom, a man of peace; but he was also a man who liked to eat; and rather than sit in a ruined house, he had joined the insurgent army, making his "X" with a flourish, smirking. His rank was that of private. He had been assigned to assist George Heritage as "explosives aide." This amused George more than it did Manuelo, who was afraid of dynamite.

Ballete could tip him, so he was willing to wait on Ballete as well, especially since it meant shelter.

The previously ebullient Calixto Ballete y Sierra was proving an exception to the rule of good-nature in camp. He could still flash his smile and twirl his spiked mustachios; but he did this like an actor absent-mindedly playing a part he had long since lost interest in. Mostly now he was glum, curt. He had not been the same man since the finding of Don Diego's body. Anxiety about what had become of Don Diego's daughter was natural enough, but Ballete carried it to the point of morbidity. At first he had been inclined to blame Manuelo, but as the days wore on, and no word came from Santiago, the young captain perversely, and illogically, turned to an attitude of suspicion of George himself. *He's in love,* George thought. He felt sorry for him; but at the same time, George watched him.

Movements over most of the camp were limited to routine. It was enough, just then, to stay alive. No such laxness prevailed, however, among those who were slated to follow Antonio Maceo in the invasion of the west. *They* worked harder than ever.

No women were to be permitted to go with this force: and that task alone, weeding out the women, was a big one. There was scouting to be done. Bridges and roads and railway tracks had to be tested, with their later destruction to be kept in mind. Supplies were assembled and sorted, only the lighter stuff being kept. Maps were studied. Ammunition was alloted. More important, for this was to be largely a cavalry thrust, horses had to be fed, cared for, trained. When George and Ballete got back to their tent at night they were tired. They didn't feel like talking, though sometimes they did play euchre. When they did this, Manuelo had to find shelter somewhere else, there being no longer room for him in the tent.

For the tent was small, and the crate of dynamite was very large: the size and shape and indeed the general appearance of a large pine coffin. Raised on a couple of logs to keep it off the ground, this crate reached from pole to tent pole. There was room at each end only for the passage of a single thin man, room on each side only for one bedroll. Manuelo, uneasily, unwillingly, slept on top of the crate. It was on this top, as it were on the coffin lid, that George and Ballete sometimes played cards.

71

Regulations called for a sentry at the tent, as a precaution against both theft and dangerous meddling, at all times when George himself was not in it. Most days this was Manuelo, armed with an old Joslyn .50/.70. The explosives tent was a center of much awed interest, and George guessed that the wily Manuelo sometimes lightened the tedium of his vigil by selling peeks inside.

George, though he said nothing about it, resented Ballete's smoking. It was not that George was edgy about the dynamite. Dynamite was his business. As he had told General Maceo, when the stuff was not capped it could be caused to explode only by some extremely heavy blow. What George objected to was the fact that Ballete smoked *cigarettes*. George enjoyed a cigar now and then, but he abominated cigarettes.

"Pass."

"I'll take it up."

Dirty stinking weeds! They made him sick, and stung his eyes in that close place, so that he turned his head a mite as he leaned forward to play a card. But he said nothing.

This was the situation when Ballete went mad.

CHAPTER XIV

ANTONIO MACEO had expressed formal regret at news of
the death of Don Diego Pineda, a man he had known before
the Ten Years War made him, Maceo, an exile. Don Diego
had been one of the largest local contributors to the war
chest; in part because his secret sympathies were with the
cause; chiefly because the rebels would have burned his
cane if he didn't pay.

But, had the *señor* found any safety fuse?

The *señor* had not. Despite a search of the house and
grounds, after they'd laid Don Diego to rest, he had come
upon nothing that could take the place of such fuse. Excepting, perhaps, these . . .

He held up five small mousetraps.

"You see?"

Maceo was not pompous. Nor did the color of his skin
cause him to smell derision where no derision was meant.
Yet he had his dignity. In ordinary circumstances rather
more than willing to laugh, he would stand no nonsense in
matters military. He didn't have time for that. Now he
stiffened, his eyes daggers.

"You will repeat that, please, *señor*."

George waggled the traps.

"Of course we can't be sure," he went on, "but it's worth
a try. Where I come from, folks have a saying that you'll
never catch a trout if you're afraid to get your pants wet."

"And just how do you propose to do this?"

"Well, we've got the caps. You only cap one end of one stick anyway, no matter how many you use. That one sets the others off. So if we can make one work, we can make them all. What I suggest is that we use one of these mouse-traps as a hammer. We set it, and we put it in such a position that when it goes off—we release it by means of a long string—then the bar that's meant to break the mouse's back comes down smackety-dab on the middle of our detonating cap."

"And that would be enough?"

"Should be. Same as when you fire your revolver. A dynamite cap's like the end of a cartridge. There's a little blob of fulminate of mercury in there, and any good sharp crack will set it off. The only thing I'm worried about in this case is that the blast will rip the wood apart and bend the wire so much that I won't be able to straighten it out and use it again. We've only got five of these things. You wouldn't want to start an invasion of Pinas del Rio with only five mousetraps, now would you?"

Maceo rose.

"We must try this thing," he said.

"No time like the present."

They made a series of tests, setting off first one, then three, then six tied-together sticks. Despite rain and some wind, each was a complete success. George, behind a boulder, set off an almost instantaneous explosion by means of a long string. He proved that the thing could be timed to a split-second. Further, he proved to his own great delight that though the wooden base of the trap was spintered by each explosion, the wire was never so badly bent, or the spring so badly sprung, that the trap could not be reconstructed.

These tests, conducted just outside of camp, created a great deal of interest. The men were amused by the firing apparatus. They had been calling George El Dinamitero or El Reventarero, but now they began to call him *El Señor Ratonera*—Mister Mousetrap.

74

George was clucking inwardly about it when he returned to the tent to find Ballete a thundercloud.

George was vexed. His good humor evaporated. He was tired of his tent companion's pettishness and silly suspicion. He had meant to tell Ballete about the success of the latest test, but a glance at the young captain's face was enough to assure him that he wouldn't be heeded. Instead he nodded only in a perfunctory manner, and started to peel off his wet coat.

"No news from Santiago?" he asked, trying to be polite.

"My agent reports that nobody like the Señorita Ana has been seen at the home of her cousins there. I think she went somewhere else."

"Must have."

There was an edge of hysteria in Ballete's voice, and it rasped George's nerves like a fingernail on a blackboard.

"Some rendevouz, perhaps?" said Ballete.

He was tense, and stared at George, his eyes very bright.

"What do you mean?"

"Señor, you talked for a long time with the Señorita Ana just before we started for the camp up here. What did you say?"

"Why, it doesn't happen to be any of your damn business, but I was thanking her for having nursed me so well; that was all."

"It was?"

George stopped taking off his coat.

"Now see here, I'm sick of this green-eyed monster stuff. Even if you were engaged to the Señorita Ana it would be bad taste."

"How do you know I am not betrothed to her? Perhaps I had a secret agreement with her father?"

George shook his head.

"That wasn't what you told me," he pointed out.

Ballete had sprung to his feet, and his revolver was out. *"Did you call me a liar?"*

George wetted his lips, or tried to. He knew now that this

75

man was not merely angry; this man was mad, he might do almost anything.

What George wished to say, quietly, in a low placating voice, was: "Nobody called anybody a liar, and now let's sit down and be sensible." But though he might have moved his lips, no words came.

He thought wildly of throwing himself over backward. But the tent wall, firmly pegged against the rain, would have held him back as though it were made of wood, not canvas.

He thought of slipping to the floor. But even a maniac could hardly have missed at that distance; and if a bullet went low, half the camp would be wiped out.

Once again he wetted his lips. He swallowed.

"Captain Ballete, *put that pistol down!*"

Ballete wavered only for an instant. Then, machinelike in the movement, he holstered his gun. He saluted the newcomer, Lieutenant General Antonio Maceo.

"Report at my tent."

"Very good, sir."

He went out.

George Heritage began to shiver. He sat down on the crate. As a civilian he could do this in the presence of a high officer; but just then, anyway, he wasn't sure whether he *could* stand.

"Thank you, general. God must have sent you."

"Not God but your orderly. He heard the voices, deduced what was happening, and ran to my tent."

"There are times when Manuelo shows a glimmering of sense."

George leaned forward, his face beaded with sweat, a touch of nausea tugging at him.

Maceo dropped a large, strong, *cafe-au-lait* hand on his shoulder.

"It's a memory now, *señor*. You won't have to see him again. He'll be transferred back to Gomez's staff. And we'll be moving tomorrow, you and I and the rest of the Sixth Army Corps."

76

George looked up.

"You mean we're going to the other end of the island? Past Havana? To Pinar del Rio?"

"To Pinar del Rio. And we'll get there if we have to swim." He patted the crate.

"I expect wonders of this, *señor*. We're through experimenting. Now we shall really blast."

"But I thought we wouldn't start until the rains had ended?"

"That," said General Maceo, "is what the Spaniards think too."

CHAPTER XV

Not with flags flying, for there were no flags to fly. but raggedly they debouched upon the plain. There might have been five thousand of them, though the number was hard to estimate by reason of the way they marched. They were scattered, never massed. Most were mounted, but their steeds varied as markedly as did the weapons they carried. Mules toted most of the burdens, hauling, too, George's crate of dynamite and the pair of four-pounders, smooth-bored saluting cannons that constituted the "artillery".

Despite weather and the lack of women, the mood of this command was one of gaiety. Men sang and laughed, or galloped from place to place visiting friends, borrowing things. A few of the more formal-minded, grouped together and began singing the Cuban hymn of independence:

Del cla-rin es-cu-chad el so-ni-do,
A las armas va-lien-tes cor-red.

Amid this holiday-outing atmosphere, George Heritage must have been one of the few somber figures. He slouched, scowling.

There were several reasons for this.

The mount assigned to him, a lank mare, all bones, was dour, cantankerous, and lazy. He named her Rozinante, or sometimes, for short, Roz. She had taken an immediate dislike to him, a feeling that was reciprocated.

With nothing to do save to try to keep dry, he was bored.

Of the sundry officers whose acquaintance he had made, none was near. Whenever George did recognize anybody, that man rode right past with no more than a wave of the hand. George might have practiced his Spanish on Manuelo, an amusing and by no means contemptible teacher; but Manuelo, though nominally in attendance upon George, was afraid of dynamite and always making excuses to fall back or to ride to some other part of the column.

More than material circumstances made George feel blue. He was in a strange country. His friends, far away, thought him dead. He was being called upon, with the threat of shameful death, to do a job he hadn't contracted for and would not be paid for. He had no rank, and could expect no sort of medal or commendation. His role was a macabre one, to say the least of it. He was, supposed, what the Spaniards called a *voluntario forçado,* a conscripted volunteer. They might laugh at him; but they had not demanded his parole. He was free to escape if he thought he could.

His position in the column during the first few days did nothing to encourage such a thought. He must have been in the very middle. On either side, before and behind, there were armed men. He was too poor a rider, and Rozinante too slow a horse, to make any dash for freedom feasible. He plodded on.

He had been issued two additional tarpaulins, making three in all, for the better protection of his dynamite. Understandably, in such weather, tarpaulins, like ponchos, were more precious than mink or sable. If even one of these was stolen, George had been warned, he would be held to strict accountability. Army-on-the-march thieves, he understood, were the foxiest of all. So he rode behind the crate.

It fitted his mood of the moment, that situation. The dynamite rested on a platform of boards, which in turn rested upon four wooden wheels. The cart was of a Biblical primitiveness, almost unbelievably noisy and slow. The crate, shrouded in three black rubber blankets, more than ever suggested a coffin—the catafalque, George called it. And despondently riding behind it, on the way to an unstipulated graveyard, through that drenching rain, he was the chief and only mourner.

Not until the third day down from the mountains did he begin to show an interest in his surroundings. On that mornning Colonel Cucasse, one of Maceo's aides, came calling.

"We have a railway, *señor.*"

"Thank God! I was beginning to believe everybody had forgotten me!"

George was swabbing his face with water. He did not need to dress. He hadn't taken off his clothes since they left the mountains.

"You want me to blast open a stretch of track?"

"That too. But chiefly the locomotive. How many sticks would it take to tear a locomotive apart, *señor?*"

"Well, now that," replied the Yankee, "depends upon the locomotive."

It was not yet light, though the east was growing gray, when they reached the track. There was only a single line of it. George didn't know where it came from or where it went, but he admired their pick of a location. This was grazing country, and the spot selected was a narrow gorge, the sides of which were stippled with palmetto scrubs. It *looked* bare, but it could hide many a man.

"Good," said George. "We can set a bundle of sticks at each end and let it pass over the first; then explode the second one in time to stop it; then go back to the first and explode that."

"A double charge right under the engine itself would be better," Juan Cucasse decided. "As I told you, the track itself means little."

"*Underneath* it? Wouldn't maybe somebody get hurt then?"

"*Señor*, this is war, not a child's game."

"But, I don't know as I'd like that."

"*Señor*, you make the bomb."

George did make it, and it was a good one. Blessedly, there was no rain just at that time, though the ground, of course, was wet. He used four sticks, tied together with strips of linen, and he capped one of these and carefully set his mousetrap. Instead of string, he had for a release line a length of wire. There was less chance that this would become entangled in the palmetto. On the other hand, it might glitter, if by chance the sun came out. It was Cucasse who thought of the glitter, not George. Cucasse walked back and forth over every inch of the line; and at the same time he made sure that word was passed among the men that nobody should approach it.

"Everything depends on that wire," he said.

For the gorge by this time was filled with rebels. They were riflemen, carefully selected. Many even had shoes. They came in threes and fours, very quietly, and took pre-assigned positions on the hillside. When the word for silence was passed, silence prevailed. All cigars and cigarettes were stamped out. Gun barrels sank from sight. Where there had been two slopes studded with soldiers, now there were but two slopes covered with palmetto.

They heard the train. It wheezed laboriously. After a long while it came into sight, warily, as though the engineer had some reason to fear just such a trap. Indeed, before it had half entered the gorge it came to a stop.

From George's point of view it was a crazy contraption, ludicrously old-fashioned. It was low, unpainted, chunky, and surmounted by one of those huge spreading stacks that had gone out, he would have thought, since the War between the States. It burned wood, not coal; there were sparks at the mouth of the stack.

There were three cars, two of them small, rickety boxcars, the third a sort of caboose with windows through which George could see the Spanish soldiers.

There might have been twenty of the soldiers. They were quiet, perhaps some of them snoozing. When the train stopped, a sergeant and a private resignedly tumbled out and started to walk along the track toward the locomotive. At the locomotive, they stopped while the sergeant talked with the engineer; then they went on walking, between the tracks now, looking down.

"Will they see it?" whispered Cucasse.

"I don't think so."

Nor did they. They walked right over the place where the dynamite had been stashed. They walked to the far end of the gorge, and, all unaware of the guns that were following their every movement, slowly and searchingly walked back to the train.

They climbed into the caboose. The locomotive chuffed sadly, and it started forward once more.

"Wait until the wheels are right over it," the colonel whispered. "I've got binoculars. I'll give the signal."

The train lurched along. It reached the tie in which George was sure he had hidden the bomb, though admittedly they all looked alike from where he crouched. It passed over this place.

The colonel's hand fell. George pulled the wire.

Each slope seemed to flatten, the palmetto fronds bending away. The locomotive reared like a frightened horse and fell back off the tracks. Incongruously the whistle blew and blew. Steam hissed skyward.

A man sprang from the woodcar and started to run.

The rebels on both hillsides opened up. The blast was terrific. The last car, the caboose, at which all shots were aimed, for a moment simply seemed to fall into splinters.

A white flag was thrust out of one of the windows. It wobbled there. Nobody fired.

Cucasse said, "I'll go down alone. Hand me the flag."

The hand tightened on George's shoulder.

"And you, *señor*, of course you will remain."

"Of course I won't."

"Eh?"

"I'm going down there and see what the effect was."

"Good. But later. When I summon you."

Cucasse was of French blood, from Martinique. This was his first field command. He was proud, his head back, as he strode down the slope, the flag of truce high above him.

There was no shot.

George wondered what had happened to the engineer. The man who sprang out of the woodcar, and who had disappeared, surely was the fireman. George hoped that the engineer hadn't been hurt.

The sergeant came gingerly out of the caboose. He waited, not without presence, for Cucasse. The two talked a little.

George couldn't see a man on either hillside. He could not see the tip of a rifle. But he would have hated to be that sergeant, the cynosure of fifty sets of sights.

Cucasse nodded, and he and the sergeant walked along the edge of the track toward the locomotive. They looked in.

The sergeant shrugged. He bowed briefly to Cucasse, and went back to the last car. Soon Spanish soldiers came forth.

They came one by one, tight-kneed, not enjoying it. They carried no weapons, and their hands were above their heads, palms out.

The whistle at last ceased to blow. The place was quiet. George started down the hill.

He knew before he moved what the performance of the dynamite had been: he knew this from the sound of the explosion, the way the locomotive had been jolted. He went not to the wheels but to the engineer's cab.

The engineer sat with his hand still on the throttle He'd been banged against the steel roof, and blood was streaming down his head.

"Make it so they can never use it again." This was Cucasse. "But for God's sake, move fast! This locomotive's got to be damaged beyond repair—and right away! That fireman only has a few miles to run to a Spanish cavalry post!"

"I'll wreck your machine for you," George promised, climbing into the cab, "but not with this man in it."

"Oh, damn it, he's dead! Blow them up together!"

"Well, maybe he's still alive."

He was. His head was cut in several places, but he was still intact, and was even recovering his senses. George got him out of the cab, shook him, and called the man with the first-aid kit before he sought out and found what was left of his mousetrap.

As it happened, he did not need to use this again. The loot made up a mixed bag: mail, raisins, wine, olive oil, six dozen pairs of socks, four kegs of nails, a thousand rounds of Mauser ammunition, a small Hotchkiss five-barr-led cannon, and a hundred pounds of No. 2 dynamite with caps *and* safety fuse.

The rest did not take long. Besides the engineer, one man, a Spaniard, had suffered a flesh wound; another Span-iard, though untouched by bullets, had had his face badly pocked by splinters. The injured were hastily treated and shoved in among the other prisoners. These were, for the most part, mere boys, badly scared. They were put to work un-loading the boxcars. George himself took charge of the dynamite, being eager to test its quality as compared with that on the catafalque. He used only three sticks, placing each in a separate part of the locomotive. He capped each, attaching a short length of fuse. Then he went to the window of the cab.

Cucasse beamed. He might have been miffed because George had insisted upon examining the engineer, but the raid was proving a sensational success. He counted the men and took a last look into the caboose and into each of the boxcars before he waved to George.

George lit the three fuses and ran to Cucasse's side.

"How long will it take?"

"Thirty-five to forty seconds—*if* that fuse is what it's cracked up to be. But I haven't got a watch."

"I have," said the colonel.

They waited, alone in the gorge now. The colonel's watch, which he held in his hand, ticked loudly. That was the only sound. But they strained their ears for hoofbeats.

"Now!" said Cucasse, and put away his watch.

The explosion came like an echo of the word. It sounded powerful, like a suppressed sneeze. The locomotive shivered.

"They'll never use that again," George said.

He and the colonel soon caught up with the column.

"What'll you do with 'em?" George asked, nodding ahead.

"Offer them a chance to join us. Some may. The others we'll kick in the rump and send them off. No sense making them take an oath not to fight any more. Their officers would force them to break it anyway. And neither would there be any sense killing them."

"But *they'd* kill *us,* if *they* caught *us?*"

Cucasse lighted a cigar.

"Why, of course," he said.

CHAPTER XVI

AT BOWDOIN, George never had been known as a literary
light. His nose was seldom found in a book. In Cuba, however, he did have one volume from which he refused to be
parted. He fetched it forth a dozen times a day.

This was the small, red Spanish-English dictionary he had
bought in Boston immediately after contracting for the
stump-blasting project. On the train to New York, on the
ship to Jacksonville, and by train to Tampa, he had pored over
it, brushing up what was left from his college days.

Not often did this fail him. But it failed on *"trocha."* It
called this simply "path." Yet what the men around him
had been talking about for many days was more than a path.
Manuelo had never heard the word. One of the officers de-
fined it as "a sort of path across a highway," which made no
sense to George; however, he was soon to learn at first-hand
what a *trocha* was in Cuba in the year 1895.

In part because of the weather, but also because of preparations by the Spaniards, who had been ready for this
move, the grand sally of the Sixth Army Corps had come to
little. It hadn't fizzled out: the force under Maceo remained
intact, its morale high. Nobody even dreamed of going
back to the Sierra Maestra, but they had been blocked again
and again by enemy columns. And so, far from having burst
into Pinar del Rio, they were still in Camaguey. Clearly it was
Maceo's policy to probe and push, darting here and there,

looking for a soft spot. At all times he avoided battle because of his lack of ammunition; he couldn't afford a pitched fight, and his men had orders to retreat after firing three rounds. Clearly, it was the purpose of Campos, the governor-general, to interpose himself in force before each such sortie. If the rebel army, or any mentionable part of it, got into the middle provinces of Matanzas and Santa Clara—the richest in the land—not only would they be able to strangle the island's economy but they would force Campos to throw a huge protecting force around the city of Havana, thus weakening his force in the field. It is considered poor strategy to risk the capture of a capital, and a hit-and-run raid in this case would have a tremendous effect upon world opinion, possibly even bringing about U. S. recognition.

As the year wore toward its close, there was shooting of some sort nearly every day. George was in none of this, though often he was so close that instinct tugged at him to duck his head. He was never alone. As a nonshooter, he had plenty of company, for by no means all of the men in this elite corps were armed. The great mass of Maceo's command, forever on the move, was kept busy at the less glorious work of burning fields and blowing up mills.

The rains had long since ceased. At that time of year—the harvest, George was told, ordinarily would start in January— the sugar cane in the fields, thousands of acres of it, was tall, dry, thick. When a torch was put to it, the Cubans called these occasions *fuegitos,* bonfires—the result, especially if there was any wind, was furious. It sounded like a terrific rainstorm, a cloudburst. The glare was orange. Night or day, and for a long while afterward, the smoke, thick, sweet, yellowish-gray, was inescapable. There were days on end, there were whole weeks, when George Heritage at all times had in his nose and mouth, in his throat and lungs, that sweet sickish odor.

His own services were spasmodically called for to blow up a bridge or a section of railroad, or to wreck some machinery in a grinding mill. He did these tasks doggedly, not enjoying

87

them. At least he never had to blow up a house. The houses were made of wood and it was easy to burn them.

All Cuba, it sometimes seemed, was covered with a pall of smoke.

They lugged along with them those ridiculous four-pounders and the captured Hotchkiss. The saluting cannons were short-barreled and couldn't fire far. The Hotchkiss was tooled for 37mm. cartridges, of which there were none.

Maceo was not often seen in camp; he was where the fighting was. George did catch him in his tent one afternoon and proposed that the guns be spiked. If anybody knew how to spike them, he said, he could do it with dynamite.

The general smiled, shaking his head.

"They are no good for their intended function, no. You can't *shoot* the things. But it means a great deal to the men to know that we have artillery. That renders us respectable. We have an army then. We are not simply bandits."

"I see."

Not the general but Cucasse took George out to see the *trocha*.

It was a bright, warm, drowsy day, like a Maine meadow in the middle of August. It made it hard for George to remember that this was almost Christmas.

He was given a real horse, a spirited black named Christobel.

"We might have to ride for our lives," the colonel remarked.

"First off, colonel," George said as they started, "what *is* a *trocha?*"

"A line drawn across a country. A fortified line. This one goes north-and-south, between Moron and Jucaro, one of the narrowest parts of the island, about fifty miles."

"Oh. The idea being to keep us from crossing into Santa Clara?"

"That's right. And into Matanzas, Havana, Pinar. We're only going to examine the southern tip of it, near Jucaro."

The ground was spongy, and the leaves of the foliage

sweated. Miraculously, or so it seemed to George, they found a path through the jungle. At no time were they challenged, nor did they glimpse or hear anything of the enemy until they came upon the *trocha* itself.

The wall was eight feet high, made of freshly fallen, criss-crossed trees. Some of these trees still had branches and leaves on them, which made the wall hard to see from a short distance.

They climbed this, and looked down, into the *trocha*.

It was approximately two hundred yards across, its width varying upon the natural obstacles present. The opposite side was protected by a tree-wall identical to the one they sat on. The floor of the *trocha* itself was studded with stumps and strewn with sawdust and with chips, as though a hundred thousand beavers had been at work. Right down the center ran a railroad track.

Before them was a square, two-story fort with a corrugated iron roof. It had a watchtower on top. There were no doors or windows on the ground floor, but entrance was gained by means of a ladder to the floor above; a ladder, George took it, that could be hauled in. The fort was made of stone and mud. On right and left, each perhaps a quarter-mile away, were other, smaller two-story forts made of mud downstairs, and with overhanging, wooden second stories.

"There's a big one every half-mile," Cucasse whispered. "We're not sure how many men they hold, but probably fifty. The smaller ones hold thirty. The fortlets hold five."

Those fortlets, three in number between the big fort and each of the smaller forts, were board structures, not strong, meant merely to be ducked into in the event of a surprise. Each looked so much like a farmer's ice house in Maine that George swallowed hard upon seeing them, and tears misted his eyes. He was back at his Uncle Eb's, where he used to spend his summers. Of all the buildings there, the ice house had fascinated him the most. He felt the same spell now. In that dank, dark, scummy swamp he still could feel against his face the air of the ice house; he could feel under his feet

89

the corky wet wood shavings, and see the rough pine beams, from which hung hams, bacon, sides of beef. The house had held an air all its own, different from anything he had known before or, until now, since.

"It is the hour of the siesta, *señor.*"

"Oh, yes."

After a while, a soldier lolled from one fortlet to another, closing the door behind him. An officer came to the ladder-door of the fort, where he lit a cigarette.

George struck the top log with the heel of his hand.

"How much of this is there?"

"About twenty miles. It goes right down to the sea. We couldn't possibly flank it."

"On the clear ground?"

"They have some logs like these there, too; but mostly they depend upon barbed wire."

"Dynamite is useless against it." He stared glumly at the buildings in the *trocha.* "One stick apiece would take those little sheds apart, but the forts look stronger."

"You wish to go over and examine one of them?"

"And get killed?"

"I mean, at night. We could just wait here till it gets dark. We have reason to think that they mean to put in calcium lights, but those haven't arrived yet. It's perfectly safe."

"You've been out there?"

"I've been over and back three times. You just have to be careful."

George looked at the dapper young colonel with a new respect. But he shook his head.

"No need. You say it's all like this?"

"Every foot. Both sides. I've scouted it clear through."

"Then we might as well report that it can't be done, not without terrible losses. The base of that big fellow out there's stone. I could jar it but I couldn't knock it down. The track would be easy, but they could still bring reinforcements unless it was cut in a dozen other places at the same time. I haven't got enough fuse. And I'd need four or five good blasters, but there aren't any in the whole army outside of me. Also this"—he hand-heeled the top log again—"is green wood; it wouldn't splinter easily. Dynamite, unless I used an enormous amount of it, might make such a mess that it would be a bigger obstacle than ever—for horses anyway."

Cucasse sighed.

"I was afraid you'd say that," he said.

"I was afraid you'd say that," Maceo said a few hours later.

He was taking a bath, his body polished copper in the light of the candle on his secretary's desk. He had been dictating while he scrubbed.

"Take another letter: To General Gomez, etcetera. 'Trocha found impassable unless forces there greatly thinned out. Suggest we meet with all our men at some midpoint—Ignacio? Cascoto?—and appear to offer battle. That might draw them. A. Maceo, etcetera.' And now if you'll forgive me, gentlemen, I'll get some sleep."

CHAPTER XVII

Maximo Gomez did come down from the hills, and he came with a rush. He commanded many more men than anybody had expected; he himself probably did not know the exact number. They scattered, grabbing whatever they could. "A plague of locusts" some called them.

Impatient with his slow-moving chief, Maceo, early in December, had assembled his men, hoping to taunt Campos into a fight—or the beginning of a fight—and in this way induce him to deplete his *trocha* force. He got more than he had bargained for.

This was near la Lechuza. George witnessed most of it, hunched under a clump of palmetto scrubs with Cucasse's binoculars, while bullets cluttered through the fronds above him. He was there by special permission of the commander of the Sixth Army Corps. "Ordinarily," Maceo had said, *"El Señor Ratonera* was too valuable to be risked. The catafalque must be kept far from the danger of stray shots, and the same applied to its keeper." But Maceo relented for this one occasion.

While he did not really ambush Campos, or even surprise him, Maceo did contrive to appear before the Spanish forces in much stronger array than they had expected. Instead of pausing to deploy his men, he attacked instantly, and ferociously.

This was not according to the rules of war, but the

Spaniards declined to panic. They formed a hollow square, cavalry in the center, and waited. They fired, but only in platoons, an eighteenth-century sort of tactic. They didn't disperse, didn't take cover. Neither did they break, though many of them fell.

The rebel fire had been scattered, sparse. The individual sounds were greatly varied, for they came from Sharps-Bouchards, Winchesters, Kennedys, Phoenixes, Colts and Wessons. They made every noise from a thin "pip" to a bass "boom." By contrast, the Spanish volleys were clean-cut, sharp, definite, businesslike. George noticed, however, that virtually all of their shots went high. The Mauser rifle had a throw lever underneath for pumping out empty shells; to work this hurriedly, under battle conditions, it was necessary to lower the butt almost to the ground, which meant a corresponding rise of the muzzle. Thus, an excited soldier tended to aim too high. This was why those bullets were snipping the leaves above George's head, though he was far back from and above the field.

"They're safer down there than I am up here," he muttered.

The rebels retreated. They did this according to a plan, trickily, holding the wings, falling back at the center. Even such an untrained observer as George could see what Maceo hoped for. Once the first attack had failed to break the Spanish column, and the rebel ammunition was almost gone, his only chance was to smash the enemy by means of a charge with machetes. This would have been suicidal while the Spaniards kept their ranks, for their bayonets were fixed and they could outreach a machete; but if Maceo could coax the enemy into an overhasty pursuit, if a few glory-thirsty lieutenants would order their own advances, then the drawn-out column could be hit from three sides at once.

The Spaniards refused to fall into this trap. Indeed, they themselves retreated. Outnumbered as they were, far from base, they could see no sense in the struggle. But they were orderly. They left the field to the rebels, but they left little else. And they remained between the Sixth Army Corps and the *trocha*.

Only if counted in casualties could La Lechuza be called a victory. Maceo edged west for several days, foraging, before reliable word reached him that Campos had reinforced his army both from Havana and from the Jucaro-Moron *trocha*, had slipped to the north of the Sixth Army Corps, and was about to confront Gomez at or near the village of Maltiempo. Maceo instantly prepared to march; but before he could get in all his scouting and foraging parties, news came that the battle had already been fought, an indecisive one.

He reversed his plan, going west instead of east. On the following afternoon, on level ground that was bare,—thanks, in part, to some grenades rigged by *El Señor Ratonera*—within two hours he took his whole force through the *trocha* near Ceballos, his losses being only two mules and a Chinese cook.

Three days later George was summoned to the general's tent.

"I thought that you might be interested in a snippet of news. Captain Ballete y Sierra was one of those killed at Maltiempo."

George rubbered out his lower lip, thoughtful.

"Was he really mad?" he asked at last.

"Could have been. There was insanity in that family. I knew his mother and his uncle. Charming, but unstable. And from this dispatch it looks as though Ballete might even have *tried* to get himself killed. He dashed right in, waving his sword and shooting his revolver."

"It sounds like him," George said.

He said it rather fondly, regretfully.

"A sergeant saw him go down. Said there wasn't the slightest doubt that he was dead. They recovered that part of the field later, before any of the villagers could strip the bodies, but they never did find Ballete."

Manuelo, when he heard the news almost crowed.

"He was a bad one, that one. For you and for the *señorita* both."

"Well, I liked him. But I'hope she didn't. At least, not too much. He was in love with her."

"Of course!"

"Umm . . ."

Manuelo flopped his arms at his sides like a tired rooster. "Ah, he's gone now."

"And I only hope that she's all right. The Señorita Ana, I mean."

"She will be all right. Wilma is with her."

This was in the tent, where Manuelo had been setting the crate with their few implements for eating. But he paused.

"All the same, if he's dead it might be well to pray for the repose of his soul, eh? If you will excuse me, *señor* . . ."

He got down on his knees.

Though jolted, as he always was by such a sight, George said "Well, if that's the way you feel about it—" He was amazed himself at going down to *his* knees on the other side of the dynamite.

Half a minute later, as they both rose, Manuelo was saying briskly: "Now shall I serve you dinner, *señor?* We have beans."

CHAPTER XVIII

WHEN HE HAD beans in his tent, he had them on a plate. When he had beans in the field, he ate them from a *jicara*.

The *jicara*, a hollowed-out ox's horn, held emergency rations, dry food. It held *boniatos*, ground corn, dessicated coconut, or *bagasse* which was dry crushed cane. The open end was covered with a tight-fitting canvas cap, to keep out rain. A *jicara* was hung from the waist of almost every man in the corps. The ordinary ones were interchangeable. When soldiers dismounted for a rest, they would unfasten their *jicaras* and toss these into the center of the circle, for consultation by anybody who was interested. Sometimes a *jicara* was passed around like a pipe of peace or a gourd of Samoan *kava*. And when the men rose to mount they scarcely looked at the *jicaras*, not caring whether they had the right ones.

The *jicara* and the machete, George supposed, were the two objects most characteristic of the Sixth Army Corps.

The machete amazed George. He had thought it no more than a cane-cutting tool; but he soon learned that the Cuban in town or country wielded his machete for many other purposes: to dig graves or gardens with, to fight with, to cut firewood with, to hack one's way through a jungle. The machete was his knife, his awl, his axe, his saber. It was a broad, two-edged, flat, non-pointed chopping piece, in size and shape somewhat resembling a Turkish scimitar. It had a bone handle, with no guard. It looked clumsy, heavy, badly balanced; but the puniest native could twirl one like a swagger-stick, and they were kept razor-sharp.

George was amused to note that most of the machetes were manufactured in New England. The most expensive and by far the best was the so-called Paraguay model. This was a product of Collins & Co., Hartford, Connecticut.

For all this, it was the *jicara,* not the machete, that brought about George Heritage's formal acceptance into the Army of Cuba.

Campos, baffled, resigned. It was an open secret that he would be succeeded by General Weyler, Spain's most thoroughgoing putter-downee of rebellion. Weyler had been active in the Ten Years War, and Cubans called him The Killer. It was understood that he would stand for no nonsense in Havana.

Maceo's men, chiefly in search of cartridges, made night attacks on Jaruco, Batabano, La Palma, San Andrea. They burned fields, wrecked mills and, enlisting men right and left, poured across Matanzas, across Havana province—avoiding the capital city itself—and into Pinar del Rio. They had little to do there. All that was expected of them, really, was to stay alive. They had shown the world that they could afford to spilt into three parts: Gomez had taken over Santa Clara and Mantazas; and Garcia had been put in command of Oriente Province. They showed that they had friends in every part of the country. They still did not control any port, nor had they taken or even attacked any mentionable city, but they were making good their boast that in Cuba the Spaniard controlled only the land he stood on. It was a good argument. It was winning many gifts. The largest gift those of the Sixth corps heard of was that brought by the gunrunner *Bermuda,* which that spring landed somewhere on the south coast of Pinar del Rio two Gatling guns, 1,000 rifles, 500,000 rounds of ammunition, and 1,000 pounds of dynamite. It was good dynamite, but there wasn't an inch of fuse with it.

There were no railroads in Pinar Del Rio, and very few grinding mills. Tobacco was the principal crop. There were many Canary Islanders, known as Islenos, and all fervently loyal to Spain; but their stores were easily looted, their houses burned, without the help of *El Señor Ratonera*. Indeed, in the camp at Las Lajas, in the hills behind Consolacion del Sur, George had some difficulty finding something to do. The New York *World* correspondent made it that much worse.

George, it transpired from the newspapers the correspondent had brought, still was a rallying cry at home: "Avenge Heritage!" "What are we going to do about George Heritage?" They were keeping his memory green, those men on the mainland who so eagerly sought to bring about U .S. intervention.

George had no official status in the Sixth Army Corps. His name did not appear on its roster. Privates and officers alike knew him only by a nickname. The *World* correspondent, who was in camp for two weeks, must have heard that nickname mentioned. Would he not become curious about this young explosives expert? Would he not smell a rat, or at least a mousetrap?

George was glad when the correspondent left, and he could get out and get some exercise.

They hit Punta Brava, Rio Honda, Consolacion del Sur, Pavo Real, Jesus Nazareno, Jamaica. That last was for one purpose only: it was near Havana, residents of which could see the flames.

Then Campos's temporary successor, Lieutenant General Sabas Marin, who waiting for Weyland, unexpectedly went into action. He darted east toward Gomez, who yelled for help.

They broke the Las Lajas camp and hurried back to Matanzas. They joined Gomez at Moralitos, and were attacked.

Both sides afterward claimed a victory, so George was told. His dynamite, and him along with it, were shifted feverishly from place to place. They had to lead every retreat.

Four days later, near the Santa Clara-Matanzas corner, the generals separated again: Gomez going east, Maceo north. Sabas had been waiting for this, and he pounced. There fol-

lowed three confused weeks of fighting, during a good part
of which time the Sixth corps was broken in half, each half
fumbling about for the other. There were battles almost every
day: Guamacaro, Roi Bayamo, Morales, San Francisco, Diana,
Rio de Auras. At last they were united, if exhausted, those
two parts of the corps. Before they could catch their breath·
they were hit first by a terrific rainstorm, then by the
Spaniards.

That was the night of March 14, 1896, which came to be
known in Cuban history as the Night of the Jicaras.

They were back in Pinar del Rio by that time, and had
flumped down in and to the north of a wood that straddled
the Candelaria highway: the general's headquarters were at
the Galop sugar mill, a structure only partially burned.

It was too early for the seasonal rains, but this one, a
drencher, was not altogether unexpected. All afternoon the
sky had been grumbling, while electricity skittered through
the air. When at sundown a halt was called the men separated
for firewood before they designed any sort of shelter. Most of
the men were encamped somewhere in the wood, but George
pitched his tent in the middle of a burned-over cane field,
far from any tree. A bolt of lightning, like a stray shot, could
set off his cargo. True, he now toted but two hundred pounds
of it; the rest, the newly arrived stuff, having been stationed
elsewhere, in the custody of Manuelo, lest a single explosion
destroy the whole supply. Nevertheless, two hundred pounds
of dynamite could kill a man quite as quickly as six hundred;
and George never did like lightning anyway.

He was not alone. Just outside the flaps he could hear men
who presumably had tethered their mounts in the wood,
themselves electing to eat in the open.

It could hardly have been later than seven, yet George,
like everybody else in camp, was so dazed by exhaustion that
he hardly knew what he was doing.

He lit a candle. And at that instant, as though by signal,
the storm struck.

It was like a squall at sea, savage, abrupt, with a great

deal of rain. It seemed to be trying to tear the earth to pieces.

The sides of George's flimsy tent whoomed in, then whoomed out again with a force that all but split them. The poles rocked. George staggered to the front flaps, it being his thought to call some of the soldiers, who could find better and nearer shelter here than the wood. He was too late. A spray of lightning made the whole world white, and he saw that the men already were running pellmell toward the trees, having left their *jicaras* behind them.

Something loomed, enormous, elephantine, as the lightning was shut off. Something bellowed.

"Mierda! Where's that damn' tent? Where's Heritage?"

"Here, sir!"

George hauled Antonio Maceo in, and tied the flaps back into place. He got the candle lighted again.

"Where are your aides?" he shouted.

"No aides," Maceo shouted. "I came alone."

"Oh . . . Uh, sit down, general. On the crate."

With dignity Maceo accepted this suggestion. He fished forth a leather case.

"Cigar, *señor?*"

"Thank you."

The general sighed, and regarded soberly the first exhalation of smoke, while the shadow of his massive figure swayed on the canvas behind him. He looked tired. To be sure. they were all dog-tired that night, but Antonio Maceo was such a mountain of strength in ordinary times that it was a little startling, even frightening, to see him sag.

"Heritage," he said at last, "you have done good work."

"Thank you, sir."

"And you haven't run away, even though you've debated it."

"Eh?"

"You Yankees sometimes think you have the—what is it called?—the poker face. But I would say that you're a very emotional man yourself, Señor Heritage."

"Say, I don't know as I like that!"

"Your pardon, then. I had no desire to offend."

"When did I ever think of deserting?"

"There have been various times. For instance, when Colonel Cucasse took you to inspect the lower end of the Moron-Jucaro line. You were sorely tempted then, eh?"

"Well, that time it was different. Some of those little forts, they looked exactly like an icehouse back home."

"Icehouse?"

"It's a place where you store the ice you've cut all winter."

"I thought that there was *always* ice where you come from?"

"Not quite always, no. But the point is, I didn't run. The colonel probably would have shot me if I had, anyway."

General Maceo held his cigar a little away from his face, scrutinizing the ash.

"Yes," he agreed. "And he is an excellent marksman."

"Well, there have been other times. I won't deny it."

"Then why have you stayed with us, *señor*, when all we can offer you is mud and peril?"

"It's hard to say. I like to work with dynamite, for one thing."

"You could do that at home, more profitably too."

"Yes."

"So then?"

"Well, it's hard to say," George repeated. "Maybe it's the place, general. Maybe it's the people here."

"Maybe it is the Señorita Ana Pineda?"

"That could be."

"That's easy to understand. Everybody loves love. But Cuba, and the Cubans, they interest me more, *señor*, right now."

George paused before he spoke again. The wind had gone, and the rain had steadied itself to a sullen thrumming, so that they no longer had to shout.

"I don't think I understand it myself, sir. I certainly never came down here prepared to like your people. But I guess I do. I guess I'd be just as bad as the rest of them. *Cuba libre!"*

101

Maceo smiled. It was a tired smile, but a fond one.

"I'm glad I came here tonight. And glad I came alone."

He took out his wallet, took out the death warrant.

"I never did hope to hold you. I kept this just in case you proved to be frightened by it for a little while. But I find that you're a man who doesn't scare easily, Heritage. Here!"

He tore the warrant into four pieces and handed these to George.

George felt foolish. He turned away, and stuffed the death warrant into his pocket.

"Why don't you join us, Heritage? I mean, formally, I can't make you a colonel. I know most of you Yankees think that down here we rate colonels a *centavo* a dozen, and that anybody who can write his name ought to be at least a brigadier general; but that just isn't so. I have only so many appointments. I can give you a captaincy."

George still was uncertain of his voice. He swallowed. He did not want to be an officer in the Army of Cuba, but neither did he want to tell Antonio Maceo this.

Just then the shooting started.

CHAPTER XIX

FOR HIS SIZE Maceo was amazingly fast. He had gone past George and was tearing open the flaps before the first splatter of sound ceased.

"Headquarters doesn't know I'm here. I must—*Ow!*"

A thud, then silence. But the Mausers picked up almost instantly, and George could hear, too, the frightened cries of men, cries that came closer. He lunged between the tent flaps.

Antonio Maceo was on the ground, groaning softly, wriggling.

The rifle cracks in the wood and on the left came closer, but George could see no flashes, nor did bullets whip the air around him.

He knelt, his hands busy.

"General, what is it?"

"My . . . my foot . . . slipped . . ."

Yes, he had trod on one of the *jicaras* that littered the ground outside of George's tent. He must have turned an ankle.

"Does this hurt?"

The fallen giant squealed; then he fainted.

That great thick-chested warrior, that nineteenth-century Achilles, had been brought low by a discarded ox horn. That fabulous figure, *El Centauro,* upon whose head a tremendous sum had been placed, lay helpless, a sack of unfeeling flesh, bone, muscle.

Men were tumbling out of the wood to spring toward the mill, or else eastward obliquely across the cane field.

"Stop! It's the general!"

They raced on like lunatics, yammering. George had seen soldiers who were frightened, but this was the first time he had seen soldiers in a panic. He cursed them.

"They're tired." This was Maceo, who had recovered his senses. "They can only stand so much. Go to headquarters, Heritage."

"And leave you alone?"

"Don't be a hero. They'll ride past. Who would expect to find the C. O. on the ground near the outside of camp?"

George looked around. There were few men in sight now, none close. From the wood came a thud of hooves and crash of branches, though the shooting itself had ceased; while around the right side of this wood, from the direction of the highway, came a brisker clop and slog. Soon the Spaniards would cross this field. They would see the light in George's tent, and almost certainly they'd take a few shots at it. *One* shot would be sufficient if it hit the crate.

"We've got to get over by the trees. Here, let me hoist you."

"You can't carry me, Heritage. I'm too heavy."

"I can try, can't I?"

"But if you'd only—"

"Shut up, sir."

The mulatto was right. It was almost a year since George's bout of yellow fever, and he had supposed himself as strong as ever; but his knees buckled, his breath vacuumed. Yet he did get the general to the edge of the wood.

"I've got to put out that candle! It'll draw fire!"

He ran back to the tent. Just before he touched the flaps, he too slipped on a *jicara*, though he kept his balance. He cursed the thing, and was about to run on, when a thought struck him. He scooped up four or five of the horns, together with their covers.

Horses had come out of the wood by now, and others were coming around the corner of it. He could not see them, but he heard them. They paused, uncertain of their whereabouts.

George blew out the candle. In the darkness he found some dynamite sticks. He found caps, and capped two of the sticks. Each of these he thrust into a *jicara*. With his crimper he punched a small hole into the top of each cover, needing the air. He lighted each, using extremely short pieces of fuse.

More horsemen came from around the edge of the wood. They shouted to one another, their voices greedily gulped by the rain.

George dashed outside, wheeled right, and threw one dynamite-filled *jicara*. He wheeled left, and threw the other. Then he ran to the place where he had left Antonio Maceo.

"Not a real attack," he whispered. "Looks like a scouting party that happened to make contact with us the moment the storm struck."

"Yet. They shot off their carbines to cover a withdrawal, and then they learned they'd brought about a rout. That's war. Confusion. But they thought fast, and decided to make a rush for headquarters. They could guess it would be at the Galop mill."

"They probably hoped to kidnap you, sir."

"They probably did. What the devil are you doing there?"

"Making a new sort of grenade."

"Wouldn't the fuse go out, in this rain?"

"Not safety fuse. Now if—"

There was an explosion not far away. They were splattered with mud.

"You see?" George said.

The explosion was startling enough, but the cries were more horrible to hear: they were the cries of hurt horses.

There was another explosion, and horses screamed again.

"Could I have your sword a minute, sir?"

"Take it out yourself. I don't want to put this pistol down."

As he drew the thing, George realized that in a year of front-rank warfare this was the first time he had touched a weapon.

It was a saber, a Toledo blade, with an old-fashioned

Cuban fingertip grip. It was very long, as befitted a tall horseman. George, who had left his crimper in the tent, used it to prick holes into the canvas covers of two more *jicaras*.

He knew what had happened, though he had not planned it that way. The explosions not only had jolted horses and riders alike, but they had filled the air with flying splinters of horn, many of which must have found their way into horses' legs.

His matches were in a waterproof box. Even so, he had to strike four of them to get the two fuses lit. Until then George had been working by feel; but now Maceo saw the "grenades."

"My God, that's a short fuse!"

"The better to burst you with, my dear," George sang out.

"Throw them! Throw them!"

"Tut, tut, of course I will."

A smoking bomb in each hand, exultantly he ran toward the loudest screams. A horse passed, riderless and out of control, nearly knocking him down. The *jicara* fell from his left hand, and he could not see it; but by fumbling he found it, and he ran on.

He stopped suddenly, and threw first the left *jicara*, then the right one. He whirled around and fell on his face.

The two went off almost simultaneously. George was showered with mud. He felt as though somebody had kicked him in the small of the back. He got up, and ran to the general. As he ran he heard on one side the Spaniards galloping away; on the other the shouts of headquarters men.

"Here!" called Maceo. *"Over here!"*

The demonstration was disgusting, George thought; yet he supposed that it was touching too. They slavered over their leader. They hugged him, and kissed his hands.

The general had been seen walking in this direction. There was a stir . . . and explosions. But there were no Spaniards now, and the men who returned looked sheepish.

They brought a litter for Antonio Maceo.

"What the general needs," Miro, the chief of staff, sternly observed, "is aides who will keep him in sight."

"What the general needs," said the general, "is a bath."

They were all there, an hour later, when reports had been made, wounds treated, crippled Spanish horses destroyed, prisoners sent off, and the camp put into some sort of order.

Clean, dry now, even fragrant, Antonio Maceo sat in a camp chair. His foot, the ankle wrapped in bandage, was on a second chair. He beamed at them.

"It was a close thing, gentlemen. The men broke . . . yes—a pity, but understandable. It was quick thinking on the part of the opposition, and a gallant try. We fight good men."

He addressed himself to George.

"Señor Heritage, I owe you much. We have no medals in this army. We have no Golden Fleece, no St. James of Compestella, or Alcantara, or Calatrava. But I did offer you, a little while ago, a captaincy. Have you decided to accept this?"

George paused only for an instant. Then he saluted, the first time he had ever done this.

"I'll accept, sir. But with a request."

"It's granted. What is it?"

"That I be given indefinite leave to go and get some more safety fuse. What I just used was the last bit in camp."

"Now, where would you expect to find safety fuse, captain?"

"Why, in Havana."

CHAPTER XX

OUR FIRST SIGHT of a storied place, if possible, should occur in predetermined circumstances. You should first see Paris on a day of brilliant sunshine—of course, in April. You should see your first Polynesian island immediately after a rain squall, when the sun, having reappeared with dramatic suddenness, glints off foliage that might be made of jade, while the jagged brown-red peaks are striped with torrents. And your initial view of Havana-de-Cuba surely should be, as was that of George Heritage, from the sea at dawn.

The whitered small crabapple of a boatman had refused to sneak in under cover of darkness, though they had the breeze.

"This is a very nervous harbor. Men shoot at shadows. But daybreak is all right. Anyone who prowls in the dark—better kill him, to be safe. But a man who starts about his business just after the sun has risen . . . why, *he's* an honest man."

They drifted, the jib sometimes giving a weary flap. The shush of sea under the forefoot was the only sound. No clock struck, no dogs barked. They slid under the grim black muzzles of the guns on the Morro, but no flag flapped at the staff there, and not a sentry paced the parapet. Havana, with its white buildings dimly shimmering, its vivid splotches of greenery, and its red rooftops truly could have been an enchanted place, something that had floated out of a dream.

Directly towards the center of this fairy city, quite as though it had been real, plodded the smudged, slatternly,

108

stinking little sloop from Rio Hondo. Heaped with fish, it was the sloppiest craft conceivable. No sentry would have hailed it. No Maine man, George was sure, would have consented to touch the thing.

Increasing the air of fantasy was the fact that George Heritage had been obliged to wait so long and to take such elaborate preparations in order to get to Havana.

He had assumed that entrance would be easy. Havana was a city in a state of siege, true, and patrolled on all sides, including the side of the sea; but a reasonably agile man surely could slip through such lines at night, or even walk through them by day, provided he was armed with a *cedula*, or military pass. There were many professional talents in the Sixth Army Corps, which surely contained at least one forger who could turn out a first-class *cedula*.

"Once in, I ought to be all right. I don't have any credentials, but in a pinch I could make up a story about having lost them. I'll get by."

He was assured that it wasn't as easy as that. Preparations had to be made. He himself, Captain Heritage, must be coached in certain things. After all, he had never set foot in Havana, was it not so?

It was. He was reflecting upon this as he drifted across the harbor, which a lightening sky was showing to be not as pure as it had at first appeared, hardly crystalline. He was reversing the usual procedure among tourists by entering the capital not first but last. Ordinarily a man visited Shanghai and then perhaps later saw something of the rest of China. Or he went to London for a week, after which he spent part of another week scurrying from point to point elsewhere in England. The preliminaries for this foraging expedition—for that's what it amounted to —had taken much longer than George expected. Things were patched, things were sent for. George must have a bag. Since he was to pose as an explosives salesman from the mainland, he must be made to look like an American again. At first he was somewhat touched by all this solicitude, but soon he remembered that

109

he could hurt the raising of rebel funds in the States only if he revealed himself. He had of course no intention of doing so. He did not take his commission seriously, for it had never been formally conferred; he had taken no oath, signed no paper. He did, however, take seriously his personal promise to Antonio Maceo, and Maceo feared that he might be recognized in spite of himself, and exposed. "Havana is full of American newspaper men," Maceo would say, shaking his head. He would say this as though announcing that Havana was full of boll weevils or tsetse flies.

As a result of all these arrangements, it was the middle of May before George got aboard that boat at Rio Bondo. Since he had first sighted the Sierra Maestra at the farther end of this island he had visited every one of the provinces. He had, however, never seen Cuba's gateway. He was looking upon Havana for the first time.

The water brightened, bits of garbage becoming visible. From the fort, behind them now, came a bugle call, reveille. Smoke lolled upward from half a hundred chimneys. The buildings were less filmy now, more garish, more solid. Persons and horses, beetlelike blobs, were moving along the Malecon. It was day.

Nobody paid the slightest attention when the sloop was brought alongside of the seawall. George, assisted from below, scrambled ashore. The fisherman, a glum uncommunicative character, didn't even say good-bye: he simply heaved George's straw suitcase to the top of the wall and pushed off.

The suitcase wasn't heavy. His clothes were neat, yet not showily new. He was clean, shaven, with face and hands tanned the color of any Cuban. Because of a map that had been drawn for him, he knew exactly where he was and where he wished to go.

He took his time. Anybody who hurried in such a place, he reckoned, would make himself conspicuous.

The streets already were astir; and he saw at once that Havana was an early-rising community. Bells were ringing. Street vendors screamed. Carters cursed.

The house was narrow, but its doorway—gateway—rather was very broad. That door was a grill, and George could see into a large, bare, empty hall, which was scrupulously clean.

The name of his man was Angelo D'Ahumada. George had been told that he could be relied upon completely.

There was no bellpull; and after some vain coughing and throat-clearing, George made bold to rattle the door.

Instantly a member of the Gardia Civile appeared inside. He held a hand on the butt of his revolver.

"What do you want?"

"Isn't this where Señor Alcatraz lives?"

"Never heard of him. This the residence of a man named D'Ahumada. Or it *was*. Right now his address is La Cabana. I expect it'll be the Laureles pretty soon. Why?"

La Cabana was the prison-fort out on the Morro. As for the death-ditch, Los Laureles, where political executions were staged, George had heard too much about that.

"Must be the wrong address," he muttered.

He went off unmolested.

He walked for some time. But he was tired, sleepy, hungry, and it was getting hot. It had been stupid of him not to insist upon an alternate base. Men disappeared unaccountably in Havana these days, he had been told.

Various offers on the part of street gamins to carry his bag he refused; and this in itself, he feared, might attract attention to him. Not that there was anything incriminating in the suitcase. He just didn't like the look of the kids.

He must get off the street. He would be logical about it. He reasoned. An old saying had it: Where would you hide a leaf? the answer being: In a forest. Also: Where would you hide a blade of grass? The reply: On the lawn. So, where would you hide a newly arrived young American businessman in Havana-de-Cuba?

There was only one possible answer.

He turned in at the bar of the Hotel Mascotte.

Though it could hardly have been much after eight in the

morning, the place was crowded, every table taken. George went to the bar.

"The *señor* will have?" asked one who was proud of his English.

"Well . . ."

"May I recommend the Jicarazo? I invented it myself."

"Congratulations. But . . . don't I remember a *jicara* being a horn that peasants carry food in?"

"The *señor* is so right!"

"Well then, what is a Jicarazo?"

"Why, a blow with a *jicara,* of course."

"You mean they hit themselves over the head with those things?"

"No, no! The Jicarazo is named after the famous bomb Colonel Ratonero invented for use against cavalrymen. Because of its . . . its . . . how do you call it? . . . it's a *keeck.*"

"Oh."

"He is a genius, that man!"

The bartender dropped his voice. Clearly it was not house policy to wax enthusiastic about rebel officers.

"You have heard of the Colonel Ratonero, *señor?*"

"Well, in a way."

"You have just come to Havana? You will hear much more."

"I guess I will. What do you make that Jicarazo out of?"

"White rum, bitters, sweet vermouth, lime juice, creme de cacao, kummel, and a dash of grenadine. It's served with a slice of pineapple and a maraschino cherry. Very smart."

"I'll have a beer," said George Heritage.

CHAPTER XXI

GEORGE HERITAGE had fallen in love with Cuba; Havana but completed the conquest. In the *manigua,* the bush, despite himself he had delighted in the flamboyant flowers, the pearly peaks, the glitter of sunshine, the gravity of night. He had not been unacquainted with nature when he came: Maine, after all, had as much glorious nature as any place you could name. But Cuba, somehow, was more than that. Of equal importance to the scenery were the grins of the Cubans, their soft voices, the way they looked at you. The Cuban, especially in Havana smiled as spontaneously as a bird sang, as a fish swam. His smile was not an extra thing a hat to be put on, but part of himself, like his nose.

In the field George had been surrounded with dedicated men. In Havana he might have been surrounded by rascals, but they were rascals of great charm. He even used to lie late in bed, a four-poster with a faded scarlet velvet canopy. Before he took his bath he would loaf there, stretching lazily, yawning, having his first cup of chocolate, while he watched the shadows from the street shuttle across the bright lemon-colored sunshine on the wall, and sniffed the roses-and-rum, the dust-and-ginger, that was always in the air.

> *Zapatero, zapatero!*
> *Yo compongo sus zapatos!*

That particular vendor, who had a boyish soprano worthy

of any cathedral, was selling shoes. They sold practically everything. This was a city with things for sale.

Me los llevo,

Se los traigo . . .

George's school Spanish tended to fall flat in this land where everything was a joke, everything had a nickname. That boy out there in the street, for instance: his cry reminded George of the name the peasants of Cuba had for the swells. These they were called the *calzados;* that is, the shoed ones, those who wore shoes.

Por poquisimo dinero! Zapatero!

Sometimes George would not get up until almost nine o'clock. Every soldier back from the front knows this feeling.

In the beginning he walked a great deal. He would stroll up one narrow street, down another, aimlessly, amiably, careful to do nothing that might attract attention to himself. He wasn't in search of information just yet. He simply was getting the *feel* of this fascinating city. His needs were few, and he did not have to worry about money, headquarters having supplied him with a fat wallet. Also, the mysterious Chinese patriot, Huau (pronounced "Wow"), would send to Gustaf Howard from Jacksonville, Florida, every second week a set sum in Spanish pesos. This would come *entrega general,* general delivery. George was Gustav Howard, of course.

The city was mortgaged to its chimneypots. The Bank of Spain dragged on, but such private houses as I. M. Borges & Co., Uppman, Hidalgo & Co., and Gelate, George heard, were sneaking funds out of the country as fast as they could. Everything was taxed. Everything depended upon sugar; and the new beet sugar competition, which was just beginning to be felt, had brought the price of crude cane sugar down to four *reales* for twenty-five pounds, or about two cents a pound. Thanks to the rampaging Gomez, precious little was getting out of the country, even at that price. Yet the Cuban could always greet you with a grin.

Once on a walk, George caught sight of the new governor-

114

general, who, flanked by horsemen with drawn sabers, drove down the Prado. Don Valeriano Weyler y Nicolau, Marquis of Teneriffe, was a shriveled man whose glittering crimson uniform, massive epaulets and rows of medals, seemed to crush him. He had small, dark lusterless eyes, and there was no color at his lips. His hands, tiny and pale, were folded in his lap. He looked neither right nor left.

Every war sucks in the cranks and crackpots, also unscrupulous persons with something to sell. No doubt in Havana there were regulations about the purchase of arms and ammunition; but no doubt, too, if you had enough money and knew the right officials you could get past these. All George wanted, presently, was fuse; but he reckoned that it was better for them to come to him. Meanwhile, bemused, he ambled. He took a drink. He went to the cockfights.

He was living not at the Mascotte but at a small, humbler hostelry on a side street; yet from the beginning it was clear that the Mascotte bar would occupy a great deal of his time. High-ceiling, furnished with large leather chairs and potted palms like the lounge of a club, the Mascotte was a headquarters of newspaper correspondents and other shady character. It was a sensation factory, a scoop plant.

Each to his own calling, George supposed. He didn't pretend to know anything about journalism; still he could not help thinking that if the people of the U. S. A. really were getting their picture of the Cuban revolt from out of this room, from these avid men, then God help the people of the U. S. A. However, he refrained from comment.

George's favorite at the Mascotte, for a week the only person he spoke to, was an employee, Mick Grito, the bartender who had concocted the Jicarazo. Micky was tiny, talkative, intelligent. He knew everybody in Havana. George wouldn't have trusted the man out of reach, but he calculated that if he stayed near Micky Grito he would be staying in the center of things, and sooner or later somebody would ask about him, perhaps circuitously approach him. He had plenty of time.

115

Micky was proud of his invention. He urged all customers to try a Jicarazo, explicating its *keeck,* and with any encouragement would babble about the great Colonel Ratonero, hinting that he knew that hero personally.

"Maybe I ought to offer to sign one for him," George thought.

It was at the bar of the Hotel Mascotte that George met Earl Bronson McPhail.

MacPhail was drunk, and he wanted to talk to somebody, but he did not trust any of the regulars; and of course he did not trust Micky Grito. He settled upon George by process of elimination.

Here was an individualist, a loner, fiercely unique. The correspondents at the Mascotte, most of them representing large New York papers, when on the trail of a scandal could be likened to a pack of wolves, howling, straining, insatiable; but MacPhail never ran with the pack. A secretive unpleasant man, habitually he hunted alone. He represented a small mid-western journal and represented it with all the energy and ingenuity at his command, a process in which the pooling of resources had no part. To Earl Bronson Mac-Phail "co-operation" was a word you could find in the dictionary, not in daily life.

He was intense, untidy, bespectacled. Tall, but stooped, he was also extremely skinny. He walked with his head thrust forward, his legs seemingly double-jointed, as though he were some gawky wading bird.

"What are you doing here?"

He might have been the head of a household who challenges a tramp in the backyard vegetable patch.

"I sell," George said.

"Sell what? Toilet seats?"

"There would be a market for them here, at that, wouldn't there?" George shook his head. "No, that's not my line. I'm in dynamite."

"Oh."

They were wordless a little while. At last Earl spoke:

116

"Speaking of dynamite, have you tried one of those Jic-arazos?"

Grito, having overheard, edged near. But George hoisted his beer.

"This will hold me for a while, thanks."

"Well, *I'll* have one then."

Micky, delighted, obliged. MacPhail grabbed the thing as though it were a baseball bat.

"You talk funny. Say, what are you? English, or something?"

"I have English blood, more or less," murmured George.

"Well, you're not a reporter anyway. That's the principal thing."

"You don't like reporters?"

"I don't like the ones around here. They'd steal the gold teeth out of their grandmothers' mouths."

He swallowed some of his drink. He glared at the glass.

"Micky named this after a bomb invented by that man Ratonero, in Maceo's outfit. You ought to be interested there, being in dynamite."

Delicately George remarked that George Heritage too had been an explosive specialist.

"Heritage? Hell, he's dead."

"Yes."

"Thank God."

"Oh?"

"Sure. If Heritage hadn't got himself executed I wouldn't be where I am now, living here in the Mascotte and with a fat expense account. No, I'd be covering scorchers and mashers and three-alarm fires."

"I see."

"But Heritage is dying anyway."

"Dying? I thought you said he was dead?"

"I mean, as a story. I don't know anything about him personally. For all I know he was probably a lemon."

"Probably."

"But even as a story he's dead now. Worn out. You've got

117

to keep feeding 'em something new if you want to make this thing roll."

"What thing?"

"Why, the cause of *Cuba libre*."

"Oh. You're a patriot then?"

"Sure. They're better copy, the patriots. But we'll never get the American public sore enough if we just keep hammering on Heritage. No, *siree*. They're sick of George Heritage."

"Guess I sort of am myself."

"Sure. You got to keep supplying something new or they'll lose interest." He leaned close, confidentially tapping George's arm. "But *I* got something for them! Got her all to myself. Yes, sir*ee*. And she's a beaut. Brother, I'm saying she's a pip!"

George said nothing, politely waiting.

"Listen, uh, what did you say your name was?"

"Howard. Gustav Howard."

"Well, listen, Howard, I mean it that this one's a peach. Smallish, but she's all there. Got tits like Lillian Russell, and the cutest little behind you ever did see. Dark brown eyes with sometimes specks of gold in them."

George felt a cold hand grip his heart.

"Your, uh, your mistress?" he asked, as casually as he could.

"Hell, no. My discovery. Comes from a high-class family, the other end of the island. They've been wiped out. Her brother was one of the ones shot at Purisimia Concepcion. Then her father was killed by the militia, and they cut up their fields and burned their house and raped her again and again—"

"What?"

"Well, maybe they didn't rape her. Matter of fact, they never got to her. She happened to be away when they came. But they *would have* raped her, if she'd been there. Right?"

"It . . . it seems plausible."

"And I ought to be able to talk her into saying that they had. Or at least that *somebody* had."

118

"Why?"

"Mister, what you don't seem to realize is that the American public *wants* rape. Murders are all very well in their place, but when it comes to getting folks really riled up there's nothing like good old-fashioned sexual assault."

"But . . . but if they didn't . . ."

"Oh, they didn't. No. But what I'm trying to get her to agree to, when I smuggle her back to the States and take her on this lecture tour, is that she'll say that they *did!* See?"

"Well . . ."

"Mister, you're no newspaper man. I can see that."

"Mister, thank God I'm not."

MacPhail had been lifting his drink a little, then putting it down a short distance away, making wet rings on the bar. He began to link these rings, quite as though he were doing some difficult chess problem. Suddenly he swallowed all that was left.

"And as a matter of fact, I don't know why the hell I'm telling you all this!"

"I don't know why the hell you are either."

MacPhail wavered. He leaned a little away from George, squinting. His eyes were red at the edges.

"Mister, I don't think I like you," he said portentously.

"Well, I know damn' well I don't like *you,*" George replied. "Why don't you get out of here?"

"Eh?"

"Why don't you comb your hair and wipe the snot out of your nose and go ahead and call on your beaut?"

MacPhail pondered this, the pulses of his temple beating, as belligerency rose and ebbed within him. He exhaled very slowly.

The bouncer hovered near at hand. Micky — his actual name was Micaelo—made wringing motions with his hands. All over the barroom there was silence.

"Well, maybe you're right," MacPhail muttered, and turned away.

Gradually, hissingly, talk started again. George took a

119

gulp of his beer, and with an elbow he signaled to Micky.

"Will he?"

"Yes. But there's no use following him. All these boys, they would like to learn his secret. Some lovely woman. If she doesn't go he will abduct her."

"Can newspaper reporters abduct people, Micky?"

"*Señor,* in Havana newspaper reporters can do anything."

"But he's drunk."

"He will slip away, *señor*. He always does."

"From you maybe. From me, sure. Or from any of these yipyapping bloodhounds. But what about Pablo over there?"

Pablo was a bartender, just being relieved, taking off his apron. He was large, square, impassive. Brushing himself, he headed for the men's room.

"Pablo, *señor?* He is stupid!"

"Yes. But he's also unobtrusive. He could get lost in a crowd of three. Save the rest of that beer. I'll be right back."

In the men's room George handed Pablo five silver pesos.

"I'll try, *señor*. Others have failed, you understand?"

"I understand that. But maybe you'll do it, Pablo. Bring me that address and you get ten more of those washers, savvy?"

"I will try, *señor*."

CHAPTER XXII

GEORGE WENT OUT, walking slowly. He bought some grapes, and went along spitting the seeds, holding the fruit away from him so that its juice would not spot his coat.

It was late afternoon, the time when you might see women in the streets, shyly slipping from shop to shop. For all the sophistication of its inhabitants, Havana must have had old-fashioned ideas about the place of women in society. Except for a few hours late each weekday afternoon, any woman you saw unescorted on the streets after midday probably was either a prostitute or a beggar. The rest might have been confined to harems.

George from the beginning had assiduously scanned every female face he passed. He had done this not in search of what Manuelo would have called a *bocadito;* that is, a tidbit. He did it because he had by no means given up hope of catching sight of the Señorita Ana Pineda.

After a while, still unsuccessful, he made his way back to the Mascotte.

"Pablo has not returned?"

"No, *señor.*"

"And Señor MacPhail?"

"Not him either."

George took his drink to a table. To cover his nervousness he picked up a copy of the New York *World* somebody had left.

The war news was the usual stuff. There was a purported

interview with Maximo Gomez, though it didn't read like Gomez to George. After a great deal of insistence that this interview was exclusive, thanks to the get-up-and-git of a *World* correspondent whose name, for safety's sake, would not be divulged (he was probably sitting in the same room with George that very minute), the story quoted Gomez as holding forth about liberty, justice, freedom. When he became specific he was funnier. For instance, he referred to Weyler as "perfectly fitted to represent the Spain of Philip II, a new Medina-Sidonia minus the Armada." The previous *World* George had seen, at Las Lajas, though it waved a bloody shirt about George himself and his "martyrdom," editorially had ventured to scold the rebels. Now perhaps because of the Hearst opposition, it thumped the table, bellowing. There was nothing too scathing for it to say about President Cleveland's refusal to lead the U. S. A. into war.

The New York *Sun,* picked up from another chair, felt that same way about the President.

"Let Mr. Cleveland be left out of sight in this debate," the *Sun* pontificated, "wrapped in the rags of his own hebetudinosity."

"I must look that up some time," George muttered.

The military dispatches, George thought, were highly unrealistic. It was an open secret around the city, for instance, that the governor-general was constructing a *trocha* from Mariel to Majena, another island "waist." Its purpose, quite simply, was to coop Maceo in Pinar del Rio, while Weyler brought all the rest of his forces against the main rebel army under Gomez. But there wasn't a word about this in any of the papers George picked up. Nor was there anything about the rumors of plots to assassinate Weyler.

On the whole, all of the papers expressed dislike of the new governor-general, and some expressed abhorrence.

"The only safe thing for Weyler to do after pacifying a district is to take out an injunction requiring that it stay pacified," the New York *Mail* and *Express* playfully pointed out.

122

"More beer, *señor?*"

"No, thanks. But you might get me a couple of cigars. Here—"

The currency, the coins, made up a nuisance. The peso was about the size of a silver dollar, and was made up of five pesetas, each worth twenty centavos. A centavo was a clumsy thick copper coin much larger than a U. S. penny. The *real,* of ten centavos, was the smallest silver coin. The smallest gold coin was the *centen,* which was worth twenty-five pesetas.

Nobody wanted the silver. All large bills were in gold, but silver coins would be accepted, as now, for individual meals or for smokes or drinks; and this was much cheaper. The small shops and street vendors seldom had any gold, and their prices necessarily were in silver, yet they had to pay the wholesalers in gold. Servants, laborers, even low-salaried clerks were paid in silver.

Draft beer was ten centavos a glass. It cost twenty-five to launder a shirt, ten more for the cuffs.

George had not yet heard from the Chinese, Huau, in Jacksonville. Doubtless that money, when it came, also would be in Spanish.

He looked up. The waiter had brought his cigars, and George was instantly aware that half the men in the room had been studying him. Heads went down as his rose. His determined effort to remain obscure had caused him to be pointed out; and his talk with MachPail had stirred even more interest.

He shrugged, returning to his newspaper. He was as edgy as a racehorse.

Earl Bronson MacPhail looked in, leering. There was something diabolic in his long horsy face. Undoubtedly he noted George's presence, and he nodded a little and went away. He wasn't walking well.

Two minutes later George looked up again, this time to see the impassive Pablo.

Pablo said nothing, simply slid a folded piece of paper

toward George, who pocketed it, thanked him, and paid him the promised additional pesos. Pablo went out.

George read a little longer. He knew he was being watched. He would not even glance at the address Pablo had given him lest instinctively he start in that direction when he went outside.

After a while he brought up a yawn. He tamped his cigar into sparklessness, paid for his beer, strolled into the lobby, chatted a bit with the room clerk, and went outside.

The Mascotte was in the middle of a block. He had to turn right or left. He turned left.

It would be light for another hour, but already the streets were less crowded. There were no band concerts in Havana at night, when men did not stroll the streets. For all its joviality, for all its air of abandon in the rowdy-dowdy blaze of noon, this city after dark could be heavy with menace.

When he had made several turnings, and was reasonably sure that nobody had followed, he slipped out the piece of paper.

The Calle de la Reina was a good street, a quiet one. He went there a roundabout way. Number Seven was two doors from a corner, and there was a policeman on that corner. George walked right past.

He didn't know why. He had not been about to do anything criminal. But he remembered how, his first morning in the city, he had called at the home of Angelo D'Ahumada and had been confronted by a plumed brute. Nobody had heard anything of D'Ahumada since that time.

George strolled a little farther, and then he turned and strolled back. The policeman no longer was there.

Number Seven was a white building of three stories. It had the usual grating, but there was a stout teak door behind this. On a brass plate affixed to this door there was an escutcheon that meant nothing to George Heritage. He yanked the bell.

The door was opened.

"Señor?"

124

CHAPTER XXIII

GEORGE WAS the first to speak, and in his own ears he sounded much as Earl MacPhail had sounded a few hours earlier.

"What are you doing here?" he shouted.

Tears leapt to Manuelo's eyes.

"You're safe, *señor!* You're safe!"

George pushed gruffly past him and into the house. He swung the door shut, still mindful of that policeman.

"Now let's make some sense of this!" He felt ashamed of himself; it was so good to see Manuelo again. "Why aren't you in Pinar?"

"I deserted." It was as simple as that. Manuelo spread his hands. "You had gone, so I deserted."

"But I was coming back, you simp!"

"After getting out, you go *back?*"

The Sixth Army Corps might have been a chain gang.

"Sure! But anyway, how did *you* happen to come *here?*"

"Why, to join my wife."

"You . . . your . . ."

Manuelo began to titter.

"Don Diego, he did not like mixed marriages. But now that he is dead we can tell. Ah, here is my wind-blown rose petal now!"

Wilma, swart, square, stolid, looked much as before. George bowed before her.

"*Señora,* your husband has just told me. Congratulations."

125

Agile, considering her proportions, she swept him a curtesy; and she too, incredibly, blushed.

"It is good to see you again, *señora*," George went on, meaning it, for there was something comforting, something of solid assurance, about that four-square undeviating figure. " And you too, Manuelo. But where . . . I mean, is it true that . . .?"

There was a step, and he turned with a glad cry.

The Señorita Ana had entered.

Perhaps because she had loomed so large in his memory this past year, she seemed now, at first sight, uncommonly small. The stair might have had something to do with this. Here was by means a large house, nor was the reception hall in which they stood ducal; but the stair had been designed by somebody with grandiose ideas. A massive thing, broad, dark, with shiny mahogany balustrades and thick newel posts, into each of which had been carved the same escutcheon that appeared on the plate at the door, it would have dwarfed anybody.

She was at least as lovely as he recalled her. "Cameo" was the word that came quickest. Her face was small, serious, delicate. Her hair was piled high and set with a tortoise-shell comb, perhaps in the hope of making her look less short; and she wore a fleecy black mantilla. She wore also an extremely tight, dark blue, silk dress. Her feet, tiny, were shod in dark red pumps. He could not see the color of her stockings, for even as she came down that spacious stair she held her skirt against flouncing.

She did not smile, but her dark, almost Oriental eyes lighted with joy. When she released her skirt at the bottom step, it was to hold out both hands, happily, in greeting.

"You are safe!"

He bent over the hands. He was uncertain whether to kiss them or simply shake them, so he did neither.

"*You* are safe!" he countered.

Then she did smile, fleetingly.

"We have much to talk about," she murmured.

126

He was to tell himself later that this was, after all, a natural thing to say; and it could even have been called unimaginative. But at the time it seemed the very peak of perspicacity. Ana was good. She was good. Kind. He knew where he stood with her. After the hushed hisses, the drinks, the false leads, the threats and warnings, the cloak-and-dagger atmosphere in which he had of late been living, she struck him as the only clean, straightforward person in the world.

"Let's go somewhere and sit down," he said.

Here again was no gem of wit, hardly a suggestion of startling originality, yet the Señorita Ana, from her eyes, took it as such.

"Yes," she said. "Come."

She led him behind the staircase and through another portal, after which, abruptly, most unexpectedly, they found themselves out-of-doors. It astounded George, who after a year in Cuba found himself for the first time in a Cuban town home more exalted than a hut. He had known that there were courtyards, open spaces, whether square or rectangular, which formed spearate rooms, family rooms; but he had never before been in one.

This was not large, (and because of the three stories it did not get much light. It had no garden, but it did have, in the center, a fountain. The fountain consisted of a basin, in the middle of which a small naked bronze boy upheld a bronze fish, laughing at it. In times of tranquillity, George assumed, water would gush out of the mouth of the fish, splashing the face of the boy; but this afternoon everything there was dry.

George paid no mind to this, for he had eyes only for his companion. In addition, he was flattered. Being asked into the court on your first visit, he took it, was like what being asked into the kitchen at home would be: it implied that you were one of the family.

He and Ana were talking on a wicker bench, their thighs not quite in contact. Manuelo smirked a little, then tiptoed away. Not so Manuelo's wife, who lugged embroidery out from under her skirts and sat in a doorway and began to work.

"I have been hungry for you," George said simply. "Tell me what happened."

It was a short story, and without shocks, for it went much as Manuelo had predicted. Ana had visited her brother's grave, that great mound, that mass depository, and while there had refrained from any exhibition of grief, merely offering prayers, lest she bring suspicion upon herself. After that, as planned, she had gone into Santiago for purposes of shopping. It was there that she had learned of the *guerrilleros'* raid on her home, and of the slaughter of her father. It had been her impulse to hurry back; and it had required all the sturdy resistance of Wilma to deter her. She had realized at last that she could do nothing, and that if she was even to survive, if the plantation was to be rebuilt, Havana must be her haven. The Hernandezes lived in Havana. She called them cousins, but this might have been a loose term. She seemed never to have doubted that she would be taken in, she and Wilma alike.

"But you . . . you have been busy! The tale of your exploits reaches us! The great Colonel Ratonero!"

"I'm not a colonel."

Softly, worriedly, she touched him.

"Whatever you are, *señor,* your head is in the lion's mouth."

"It's been there before. Now tell me about yourself."

Life was dull in Havana. Two or three mornings a week, Wilma trailing her, she might go to mass; but she never did go for a stroll, or to the market. Her brother, it transpired, had contributed heavily to the cause of *Cuba Libre,* and in more ways than one. It seemed safest for the Señorita Ana to stay under cover. If she were gone the land was lost; and it was clear that, for all her genuine grief, she never lost sight of that land. Watching her, listening to her, George wondered: was it an aristocratic tradition, or the earth-greediness of a peasant? He didn't know, and did not really care.

"It must not be taken away! I must hold it somehow!"

"Yes."

The courtyard, deep like a well, had grown dark, though it was but dusk outside, as the sky showed. Wilma put her embroidery aside and lighted a candle as thick as her own Amazonian arm.

So the Señorita Ana had remained indoors, chafing. She came from a country province, where it was no disgrace for a lady to ride forth. And at home she had ridden. Without Wilma for company she had climbed the hills. She was absorbed in the cultivation of cane, and had helped her father to supervise the cutting and grinding, the sackage, even the hauling-off, for she could haggle over prices and tend the hands as she bossed the house servants. She could ponder what to do about the slopes, which were too steep for cane, and no good either for the cacao trees that had interested her father. Good land, rich red-brown earth, was going to waste.

"Pineapples," George snapped.

"Eh?"

"They'll grow anywhere on a hill, no matter how steep it is. A planter in Pinar told me so. They don't cost much either."

"But they are a Cuban fruit. They'd have no market outside."

"Maybe a market could be built for them? But . . . go on."

It was not likely, the Señorita Ana reflected, that the government would search her out; but it was as well not to tempt fate, not to push her luck too far.

"Yet *somebody* sought you out."

Startled, she looked at him.

"You?"

"No, not me."

She never thought of lying. He could see that in her face. He turned away, studying the shadow of the little bronze boy.

"The Señor MacPhail. How did you know?"

George shrugged.

"We live in a whispering gallery here," he mentioned.

"He came one day last week. Then he came again and

again. It was a treat to see anybody, and to practice my English, which is not good."

"Your English is excellent."

"But I did not like him. He wishes me to sneak out of Cuba with him, to meet many people on the mainland. He says it will help the Cause."

"It could. But it would make a fool of you. And it would put your picture on the front page of every paper in the States. And wherever you went people would slobber over you and ask for your signature."

"Oh, no. I would never sign my name to anything I had not read carefully first."

"Good girl!"

"He came again a little while ago, that American."

"Yes, I know."

"He was drunk."

"I know."

"I wouldn't see him. I sent him off. I . . . I don't know what to do about going with him. I am not happy here, and If I could truly help *Cuba Libre* I'd do anything . . . anything . . ."

"No," said George. "It would be wrong. You must not go."

"Yes," she whispered. "Gracias, *señor.*"

George, who had been about to apologize for his posseeiveness, changed his mind. He only nodded, as though *that* matter was settled. He rose, feeling good.

"Well, I guess I ought to go. Hate to."

All three of them, for Manuelo had shuffled back, accompanied him to the entrance hall, to the door. Ana extended her right hand, palm down, and this time he *did* kiss it.

"Please come again," she said.

"Tomorrow!"

The street was deserted and dark. Not even from a distance could he hear the clop of hooves, the click of heels.

Cautiously he went to the corner. There was no reason for this. He mustn't permit himself to look furtive! Nevertheless, he glanced right and left.

130

He was about to start in the direction of his hotel when there was a step behind him. A shadow emerged from a doorway, a hand fell upon his shoulder.

"Señor Gustav Howard, you will come with me, please."

It was the policeman.

CHAPTER XXIV

INSTINCT TUGGED at him to fight, or to run, but he resisted this. Either course might prove too great a temptation for the burly man who faced him. The cafes of Havana buzzed with stories of prisoners who had been killed while "resisting arrest."

George might have blustered. But the cop had a gun, and he did not look like a man easily swayed. So George simply nodded.

"All right."

They turned to the left, George, as they walked, tried to remember whether there was a police station that way; and he could not think of one. Was he being taken to something other than a police station? Was there some specially equipped questioning-chamber? He walked on. He would have tried to whistle, but feared a failure might make him ridiculous. The policeman walked half a pace behind.

The lights of the Mascotte swam into sight, and with them the sound of the Mascotte bar voices:

When you hear dem bells go ding-a-ling,
All join 'round, and so loudly you must sing . . .

George sighed. No opera-goer, he never had heard de Reszke, Tetrazini, Schumann-Heink, Scotti; but he doubted if all four together could have produced music that would sound so sweet to his ears just then.

And when the verse is through, the chorus all join in:

There'll be a hot time in the old town tonight!

Yet they did not pass the Mascotte as he'd expected. Directly before its door they stopped, the policeman facing George.

"Here we are, *señor*."

"Why, yes."

"The Señor MacPhail, he wished to speak to you. He is in Room Two-o-Two."

Relief soothed George's nerves.

"Oh? And who does MacPhail think he is that he can send flatfeet to fetch people he wants to see?"

"I do not know, *señor*. But I know he is in Two-o-Two."

"Well, not your fault. Thank you, officer. And, good night."

"Buenas noches, señor."

But the cop didn't go. He just stood there, beaming. And George, with a gulp of indigation, handed over three pesetas.

"Gracias."

"Don't mention it."

The policeman actually bowed. Mockingly George bowed back. Then George went into the hotel, a free man, feeling very foolish.

The boys in the bar-room, on his right were giving forth another familiar number:

> Hail, hail, the gang's all here!
> So what the hell do we care?
> What the hell do we care?
> Hail, hail . . .

The room clerk said that the Señor MacPhail was sick.

"He'll be sicker when I'm through with him. Give me a key."

Earl Bronson MacPhail had indeed been sick, and recently —in a porcelain washbasin on the floor. The room was filled with the sour smell of his vomit. He himself lay in the bed, groaning.

"Never should drink . . . never . . ."

"Stop feeling sorry for yourself. I'm here. What d'ye want?"

"Oh, Howard . . . I sent for you."

133

"To clean up?"

"Don't be sarcastic. Can't stand it. No, I sent for you because I wanted to apologize. Lost my head. Shouldn't ever drink."

"Well . . ."

"Fact is, I got so lonesome . . . *ow!*"

He floundered off the bed, and made for the basin, where he was sick again.

George stepped back.

"Wanted to apologize," MacPhail went on, after he had washed his mouth, "and congratulate you. Only man in the place could have thought of Pablo. I spotted him as I came out. Too late then. But when I heard he'd reported to you I wasn't surprised. That's why I gave the copper your name. All the same, Pablo never could have done it if I hadn't been soused. Sit down, Howard."

"No, thanks. I don't mean to stay long. This place stinks."

"Sorry. I'll make it up for you. Especially if you can get my pippin back. Talk her into going to the States. She turned me down."

"No," George said. "I won't do that."

"Oh? You don't support *Cuba Libre,* eh?"

"I like *Cuba Libre* all right. But it's one thing to fight for what you believe in and another to step into the bowwow box and bark for patriots at so much a sucker."

"Them's nasty words, Howard."

"Maybe I'm in a nasty frame of mind."

MacPhail sat on the edge of his bed, put his elbows on his knees, his head between his hands, and rocked back and forth.

"Nix, nix. Don't gravel me. I said I'd make it up, didn't I? Anyway I've got another scoop ready for those Little Lord Fauntleroys downstairs. Exclusive interview with Weyler."

"Good God! How did you ever manage that?"

The governor-general abhorred correspondents, none of whom, as far as George knew, ever had succeeded in getting

134

an appointment with him. But then, it was MacPhail's custom to do the impossible.

"Look. In my coat there. Week from Wednesday. Three-thirty. Just before his bath. Signed by Colonel Escribano himself."

George found the paper. It was signed, sealed, stamped. The time and date were as MachPail had said; only MacPhail was to be admitted to the palace. The interpreter, it was stipulated, should be supplied from the governor-general's own staff.

George put the thing back. So MacPhail didn't know Spanish? And he was a drunken sot. Yet he could obtain a privilege like this! But aloud, George was down-to-earth.

"Now, what about that favor you mentioned?"

Bleary, soggy, MacPhail looked up. He studied George for some time, a scrutiny in fact not easy to bear. Nausea, headache, and all, Earl Bronson MacPhail was a formidable examiner.

"You know, Howard," he said at last, "you never did tell me whether you were interested in *buying* dynamite or *selling* it."

"Maybe it would be just as well if you didn't know."

"Maybe. Well, either way Pappachristides is your man. But don't mention my name."

"I see. And how would I meet this Pappa-whatever-his-name-is?"

He comes to the bar downstairs every Wednesday afternoon. Always sits in the back, far away from any window. You can't miss him. Now how 'bout going away and leaving me to my misery?"

"What you need is to sleep."

"What I need is to die," said Earl Bronson MacPhail. "But I don't think I'll have such luck."

In the morning, as chipper as an October squirrel, George over his chocolate, papaya, and omelet, counted his money. He had twenty-seven pesos left. He owed his hotel almost that. It remained for him to go to the main post office and see if his expenses had arrived from Jacksonville. This he was reluctant to do until it was absolutely necessary. There could be some risk involved; and this morning at least he was feeling much too good to mix with risks.

Instead, he bought a new linen suit, waiting in the tailor's shop until it had been altered to fit him; then, having still a few gold coins left, he put the suit on, bought a new hat, bought two dozen long-stemmed red roses and, for his buttonhole, a gardenia.

Whistling *Hot Time in the Old Town Tonight,* he went to No. Seven Calle de la Reina.

CHAPTER XXV

HE WHO HAS KISSED a knave (an old saying goes) should count his teeth. George had no intention of kissing the toad-like Nikos Pappachristides, but if their deal was to be completed, and they were to shake hands, he'd certainly count his fingers afterward.

Pappachristides was chalk-white, dry. He never looked at you. He spoke, when he spoke at all, in a raspy lisp.

In the Sixth Army Corps, after a fight, cigar ash often was used on open wounds. It was supposed to help avert gangrene. Whether there was any foundation to this belief George did not know, and didn't care; but his first thought when he met Pappachristides was that this looked like a litter case.

For the man attracted dust as a magnet did steel. He was neat and precise in his movements, even rather prim and— oldmaidish. The ash from his very thin, very expensive cigar, which he smoked with the air of a high priest who conducts some sacred rite, each time was carefully knocked into a tray. That which covered him like a fine volcanic grit seemed to have solidified in the air, forming itself as raindrops do. When he stirred, rivulets of it ran down the creases of his coat. His very mouth seemed sanded with it. And George had no doubt that any shampoo would wash a bowlful of the stuff out of that unshining thick, black hair.

At their first meeting nothing had been accomplished.

Pappachristides never had turned his head, much less his eyes; yet George distinctly had the feeling that he was being studied, appraised. In time, and almost as though he had heard nothing, the Greek rose with a sigh. As he turned away, he murmured something about the Cafe de Jesus tomorrow. That was all.

At the Cafe, to which George obediently went, more was done. There Pappachristides, though he did not admit that he might be able to find some safety fuse, at least didn't deny this possibility. However, he would not talk price. To the shocked indignation of George Heritage of Androscoggin County he insisted, if apologetically, upon first seeing the color of George's cash.

"You don't *trust* me?"

"Of course, *señor*. But . . . this is wartime."

George had no money, and he had been obliged to let Pappachristides pay for the lunch. But afterward, having put it off as long as he could, longer than he should have done, he braced himself for a visit to the main Havana post office, to the *Entrega General* window.

Moreover, George, three weeks in Havana now, had reported only once, and that time informally, indirectly. By means of the fisherman who'd brought him, George had sent to Antonio Maceo personally not a message but a box of good pale cigars and a flask of the best obtainable French perfume—gardenia, the general's favorite. For the rest, the men at Sixth Army Corps headquarters might have thought him dead, truly dead this time. They had plenty of dynamite; and before he left camp George had trained several officers in its handling and use. But they had no fuse. That was up to him.

So he went to the post office.

There was not the slightest hitch. His broken Spanish caused no comment; the clerk scarcely glanced at him; and he was not required to show his credentials, though he did have to sign a receipt. Two minutes later, with, as far as he knew, nobody watching him, nobody following, he walked out

138

of the post office, an international money order for five hundred pesos in his pocket.

At the Bank of Spain, too, things went smoothly. They did take his address there, and they did ask to see his (forged) credentials. They gave him a receipt for the money order, imploring his pardon for the delay, and told him that they would send a messenger to his hotel within one hour. George guessed that it would have to do, and he left.

He had an anxious time at the hotel, jumping at every step; but the promised messenger, togged out in a uniform that impressed the proprietor, duly arrived. George was called downstairs, where he counted the money and signed still another receipt, handsomely tipping the messenger, who bowed to him. Then George paid his hotel bill and, having no appointment with Nikos Pappachristides until the following noon, bought three dozen carnations and went with them to No. Seven Calle de la Reina.

It was a curious household. Señor and Señora Hernandez he never did see, though he had no reason to doubt their existence. Hernandez, he understood, was some manner of merchant, and judging from the furniture and appointments of his house he did very well in his work. He and his wife, politically conservative, as so many merchants are, might have been unsettled by the visit of their country cousin, whom they might have begged to stay indoors. They might have been even more embarrassed—if they had known who he was—by the visits of George Heritage. Bluntly, they could be avoiding him, preferring not to meet him, and to remain officially unaware of his presence, against the chance that they might be called upon to give testimony concerning him. Now and then, seated in the court yard, where he was always received, George would hear a footstep or a softly closed door upstairs, but this could have been caused by a servant.

He and his hostess chattered in the court like a couple of monkeys, each amazed to find the other, and himself, so loquacious. Manuelo came and went, grinning fatuously; but

139

Manuelo's bride always was there, working at something, yet keeping her ears cocked. Though sometimes he would hear sounds from the kitchen, it was seldom that George saw any other servant. He never was asked to stay for a meal. On the other hand, the door invariably was opened at his knock.

The Calle de la Reina was a quiet thoroughfare, and No. Seven contained a quiet household, with nothing furtive about it, nothing sneaky. But all the same, George was troubled about the welfare of the *señorita*. He stewed.

"Manuelo ought to have a pistol."

"He'd be afraid to hold it, much less shoot it," Ana said.

"Well, I'm going to get him one. Tomorrow I have lunch with a certain foreigner who deals in such things, and I'll buy a gun."

"You don't carry one yourself, *señor?*"

"No. Never have. They can get you into trouble."

The Señorita Ana weighed this, her eyes thoughtful. When she spoke it was carefully, not in the least cockily; yet George was irritated.

"If it is my safety you think of, *señor,* wouldn't it be better to buy *me* a gun?"

What rankled about this remark was the realization that it was sound. Manuelo would jump at the sight of his own shadow; whereas his mistress, tiny though she was, could be cool in any emergency. It never ceased to amaze George that this delicate creature, at first sight all fan and mantilla, all rustling silk and downcast eyes, could ride like the wind and shoot like a master. She looked a figurine of painted porcelain, but she had the heart of a huntress.

George was short.

"I'll buy it for Manuelo," he said.

In the entrance hall, Wilma approving, George kissed both of the girl's hands, as had been his wont each afternoon when they parted. He would have preferred to kiss her mouth, but he was yet unsure of himself, fearing to overstep his welcome. Their relationship was a curious one. Starting with a muffled and mistaken kiss in a dark lane, it had passed

140

through confusion to mutual suspicion, but now was moving toward companionship. This past week, during the hours in the court, each had told the other about his childhood, his family, and hopes. Yet they had been grave about this. They never simpered or giggled as other lovers did. They called one another *señor* and *señorita*. George *thought of her as Ana;* but he wouldn't have ventured to *call* her that.

Nikos Pappachristides was trying that next noon. Nevertheless the deal was made for what George termed scandalous prices. The Greek, in the baabaa bleat of his, constantly reminded George that this was wartime. George supposed that logically he should not care what he spent, so long as he got the fuse, and so long as he saw to it that the said fuse was turned over to that dour, shriveled little fisherman at the sea wall along the Malecon some morning just after dawn. That was, George gathered, what war was—a time to be gouged, and to gouge the other fellow in turn. Dirty.

When a revolver was mentioned. Pappachristides for the first time showed a touch of astonishment. This was not because he was unacquainted with the custom of lagniappe, but because of the nature of the article.

"I want it for a friend," George made clear.

Pappachristides had no use for gifts, excepting such as might be given to *him;* but he was ever ready to make a sale. And by this time he trusted George. With a hand as pale as it was small, he reached under his coat and drew forth a .38 Colt self-cocker, a Navy model, nearly new and in perfect condition. Coming out of him, it was as unexpected as though a rabbit had barked or a guinea pig had snarled.

He placed this pistol on the bench between them in such a spot that nobody save a person who leaned over both their shoulders, standing directly behind them, could have seen it.

"Twenty pesos, *señor*. I *paid* that for it. Besides, it's loaded."

"A deal."

The gun, though somewhat heavier than one George himself would have selected, fitted easily into a hip pocket. Not so

141

the fuse, which was contained in a bulky cardboard carton. George left the fuse in his hotel room when he went to No. Seven Calle de la Reina that afternoon. He didn't like to do this, but he could think of no other place for the package. The hotel didn't have a safe.

He forgot the gun in his pocket when he met Manuelo. Perspiring, his lips working, his eyes bugging out, Manuelo looked like one who had seen a ghost.

"For God's sake, what is it?"

Weakly Manuelo motioned for George to follow. Manuelo was so distraught that he forgot to shut the street door; George shut it for him.

They went to the court, and there George saw the reason for Manuelo's manner. He *had* seen a ghost.

For seated on that same wicker bench, side by side with the Señorita Ana Pineda, upon whom he flashed his white-toothed smile while his palms stroked his knees and his shoulders quivered with exuberance, was Calixto Ballete y Sierra.

CHAPTER XXVI

THE FIRST FEELING George had was one of resentment. Ballete, leaning toward her, twirling his mustachios, was so
confoundedly sure of himself! Though dressed as a civilian,
indeed a dude, figuratively he still wore his military boots,
still had sword at his side.

"Damn it, what are you doing here?"

Ballete sprang to his feet, ignoring, or it could be not even
noting George's rudeness, his vehemence.

"Amigo!"

He seized George's hand in both of his and pumped it.

"You can't do this," George said, modifying his tone, for
he was somewhat ashamed of himself. "Don't you know
that I have already prayed for the repose of your soul?"

"You did?"

"Well I guess I shouldn't've."

Tears came to Ballete's eyes, broke there, and coursed
unabashedly down his cheeks. He continued to shake George's
hand.

It was not possible to resist him. George smiled sheep-
ishly, returning the handsqueeze; yet at the same time George
was wary. If this overemotional youngster thought to disarm
him by turning on charm—well, he had another think coming.

Ana could conceal fear like any queen; yet her relief at
the sight of George this afternoon was too much for her,
and she all but ran to him, crying out.

143

"You're supposed to be dead," George admonished Ballete, trying a playful approach. "You know . . . dead. Like me."

"No, no, I simply deserted!"

"Now, what in the world did you do that for?"

"I was bored. When you went off with Maceo they made me stay behind for staff work. I was a glorified messenger-boy, so I deserted."

"I see."

The Señorita Ana instinctively had moved away from Ballete, in whose eyes a crazy light shone.

"I was just beginning to explain to the Señorita Ana here . . . Ah, I see that you two know one another?"

This really did frighten George. Ballete was not hiding anything. He truly had forgotten that the last time he faced George, some seven months ago at the other end of the island, it was with drawn pistol and in a rage of jealousy over this very girl.

"I was explaining that I had not quit the cause. Ah, never! But Gomez is too slow. *I* am taking direct action, on my own."

"Sit down," George tried, "and tell us about it."

"Gracias. May I, *señorita?"*

The court never had known a stranger scene. Behind latticed doors, at least Wilma and Manuelo, and probably others, listened to the tale. George at one end of the bench, the Señorita Ana at the other, sat stiff as pieces in the Eden Musee.

Ballete himself, in the middle, was quite at home. Elegant, affable, with his best drawing room manner, he might have been balancing a cup of tea, chatting with a duchess or two.

He had, truly, dashed into the fighting at Maltiempo. But he hadn't been wounded, much less killed. He had bribed a sergeant to report his death. It had been an occasion, fairly common in this war, when each side was in retreat, uncertain of the strength of the other. For a little while Ballete had had the field to himself. He had hidden, he didn't say where; later he'd walked off.

144

"I wished to get to Havana," he told them. "But I was delayed."

How? Had he wandered the countryside for months? Had he holed up with friends, of whom he had many, all wealthy? Had a disease brought him down? Except for a feverish flush of the cheeks and an overbrightness of the eyes, both of which symptoms could have been accounted for by excitement, he looked healthy enough now.

He had been delayed, but at last he'd reached Havana. Yet he still had them. He had carried them through everything.

"Carried what?"

"Ah, *amigo,* it pains me to tell you, you who have been so kind to me. It pains me to tell you that I robbed you."

"Hell, I haven't got anything to steal!"

"The dynamite."

"Eh?"

"When I went back to our tent to recover my effects, before I was transferred, I took two sticks from the crate. I also took a cap. And I carried these with me all the time."

"You mean you went into *battle* with them?"

"Ah, yes. Everywhere I had them. I had watched you. I knew how to put the cap on. And I kept them in my pocket until this morning. But they are in a better place now."

He leaned back. He wanted somebody to ask where those dynamite sticks were. But George had another question first.

"How did you ever find your way here?"

"To this house? Oh, I have relatives in Havana. They harbor me. And I watched for the servants of friends, at the market."

"Bright," said George.

"Yesterday I saw Wilma, and I followed her here. But I didn't come rapping right away. I had other work to do first. I had the bomb."

Ana was rigid, but George sprang to his feet.

Ballete, pleased with the effect of his announcement, smiled.

"I tied the two sticks together and capped one of them and

145

put them into a tin box. Then I filled the empty space with nails, and put the inside of an alarm clock at one end. When the alarm goes off, it will strike right in the middle of the cap. Then—boom!"

"Yes," muttered George. "Boom."

"It is fixed for ten minutes after four." Ballete drew a watch, and consulted it sagely, nodding. "Fifty-three minutes. We should be able to hear it go off from here."

"Good God, where is this thing?"

"Why, in the bathroom."

"What bathroom?"

"The big blue-tiled one at the palace, the governor-general's private one. He takes a bath there every afternoon at four. Everybody knows that. But I paid well to make sure. Almost as much as I paid to get in there this morning and hide the thing."

He beamed, looking from one to the other. It was obvious that he expected applause, cheers, slaps on the back.

George extended a hand toward the Señorita Ana.

"That's mighty interesting. But right now, won't you excuse Señorita Pineda and me for a minute? It . . . it's private."

The young man darkened, and his hand twitched close to his lapel. It was likely that in the dark, disordered recesses of his mind some memory of a past rage lurked, pressing out.

"Private?"

Into his eyes came the same tight, hot expression as when, a moment before, he mentioned the governor-general.

"Just a second," George said pleasantly.

He lifted the girl to her feet. For all her self-possession, he suspected that behind that skirt her knees were quaking. He led her across the court. He could hear Ballete's heavy breathing. He didn't know what he'd do if Ballete drew a revolver.

The instant the door was closed behind them he grabbed Ana.

"He meant that! There *is* a bomb there!"

146

She wetted her lips.

"I haven't any doubt of it," she whispered.

"We've got to prevent it!"

"Why?"

This was in half-darkness under the staircase, and he gawped at her, unbelieving.

"Why should we save General Weyler? He's a brute, and he deserves to be blown to pieces."

"Oh, I agree there! Sure! But can't you see what it would mean? It'd end any chance of help from the mainland. The Yankees, all my countrymen, they'd be disgusted. It'd slam the lid on the war chest."

"But why should your Yankees object if we want to assassinate our governor-general? Isn't that our own affair?"

"Yankees don't always look at things that way. No, we must stop this, somehow. I've got to get word to the palace."

"You can't go there! You'd be arrested!"

"Yes. But I happen to know a man who *is* going there this afternoon anyway. But I can't leave you in this house. Here—"

He swung the door open and shoved her through. She did not resist. She might even have enjoyed being pushed.

More than one pedestrian looked askance at them as they dashed through the streets to George's hotel, where the manager gave a broad significant wink when George demanded his key. The clock in the lobby said three-sixteen. They sped up the stairs.

"Wait here for me," George panted. "And lock the door."

The manager in the lobby looked dumbfounded when George ran outside. The clock said three-seventeen.

There was a four-wheeler before the Mascotte, an exceedingly expensive hack drawn by a pair of smart chestnuts, and just now occupied only by the driver, who clearly was waiting for somebody.

George did not even ask at the desk for Señor MacPhail. Instead, knowing the way now, he ran to Room 202.

The door was ajar. The smell, the dissheveled scene, were

147

the same as they had been at the time of George's previous visit. He stared, bewildered, truly thinking for an instant that something had happened to time, causing it to reverse itself.

There was the coat thrown over a chair, a basin filled with vomit in the middle of the floor, and a whiskey bottle on the washstand. Sprawled on the bed, shoeless, tousled, mumbling unintelligibly, was that irascible, unpredictable scoop specialist, Earl Bronson MacPhail.

Whether he was drunk again or drunk still, indubitably he was drunk. He had forgotten his hard-won interview, forgotten the carriage.

George stood over him a moment, weighing the chances of shaking, cold water, or yells. He decided against these.

There was one other bet.

The notice of appointment, with all its seals and stamps and signatures, was intact in an inner pocket of MacPhail's coat. It contained no description of the man to whom it was made out. Conceivably the guards, the aides, and secretaries, did not know, by sight, the celebrated Señor MacPhail.

At least the carriage driver didn't, for he made no protest when George jumped in.

"The palace! Fast!"

Clocks all over Havana were striking the half-hour.

CHAPTER XXVII

IT WAS A LARGE stone building in the Plaza de Armas, weather gray, ornate, and somewhat smudged. An iron fence surrounded it, and George's first stop was at one of the two main gates. The guards there gave little trouble, being awed by the order of appointment.

The guards at the door were more finicky. The *Yanqui,* they declared, must be searched. It was regulations.

This rocked George, though he should have anticipated it. The pace of events had given him no chance to reflect that, what with assassination stories floating around, the palace guard would naturally insist upon a search of all visitors.

If there was nothing on George's person to prove that he was Earl Bronson MacPhail, neither was there anything to indicate that he was George Heritage, or the fabled *Ratonero.* But there *was* the revolver he had bought from Pappachristides. It hung like lead. He marveled that he had been able to walk with so much weighing him down. And it must have made a monstrous lump on the back of his coat.

There was something else, in another pocket, that could prove damning not only to him but to Ana Pineda. It was his hotel key. If they took this from the person of a visitor who had also carried a revolver, they would go to that room and find Ana and six hundred feet of safety fuse.

"Search me?" he cried. "Of course not!"

His first thought was to retreat. He might hurry back to

149

the Mascotte, on the plea that he'd forgotten his pad, and leave the pistol and the key there. But they might hand him a pad and a pencil. More important, the clock in the grand entrance hall said twenty-six minutes of four. He was already late for MacPhail's appointment. And he did not even know where the blue bathroom was.

"Say, I'm a U. S. citizen," he cried. "You're not going to strip me in front of all these men! I won't stand for it!"

The captain spread polite hands.

"*Señor,* there is no thought of stripping anybody. It is simply that we would feel here and there about your cloth-ing—"

"Absolutely not! Stripping is what I call it, and that's what my paper would call it too! An insult to an American! D'ye think all those others"—he waved in the general direction, he hoped, of the Hotel Mascotte—" wouldn't get behind us in a campaign like that? Why, of course they would!"

Though he had forgotten the Colt, George had thought of one touch of which he now felt proud. He'd taken a swift swig of MacPhail's whiskey, for effect. He wished to smell as much as possible like a war correspondent.

Now he thrust his face into that of the captain of the guard.

"So why don't you go ahead! See what it gets you! That's all they need in Washington is another martyr like George Heritage!"

The captain sighed, and stepped back, and sent a soldier for a superior, with whom he consulted in low whispers. There was a great deal of shrugging; and at last the captain signaled to George.

"Very well, *señor.* If you will come this way—"

The clock on the wall said twenty-two minutes of four.

The staff was efficient. George had feared a series of under-lings, the filling-in of many forms. Nothing of the sort held him up. He was introduced at once into the office of Colonel Escribano, a pudgy, scrupulously courteous little man.

"You are late, *señor,*" Escribano said in English. The

appointment was for half-past three. The governor must end it by five of four. He takes his bath at four."

"So I've heard."

"Well, I'll send for an interpreter."

"Don't bother. I think I know your lingo good enough to get along."

Escribano rolled up his eyes froglike.

"The order of arrangements made no mention of Spanish."

"A slip," George said airily, "on the part of my secretary."

"I see. Well, we can be about the business right away then."

Don Valeriano Weyler y Nicolau was a squinched-up man with dark, murky skin, black hair, and eyes the color of sherry. Those eyes were set far apart, as his ears were set far back on his head, and though his whiskers were lush he wore no hair on his chin. It was a truculent chin, and sharp. For a soldier he was singularly sloppy, a figure altogether different from the bemedaled, befeathered one George had glimpsed on the Prado. His linen was clean, if rumpled, but his creased black alpaca suit might have been taken from any sixteen-dollar-a-week bookkeeper. His fingers were not ringed, and there was no ribbon in his buttonhole.

"You are late, Señor MacPhail. You may sit down."

George felt a chill take him, then release him.

"It is well that you comprehend Spanish, *señor*. It saves us time. You know, of course, that the new *trocha* cuts off Maceo and his so-called Sixth Army Corps entirely?"

He spoke a Castilian so stilted, so pure, that George, with his own limited, slap-dash Spanish, had difficulty understanding him.

"It eliminates them," he went on. "And it will obliterate them."

"Obliterate?"

"Not today, nor tomorrow, but soon. It would not be discreet if I told you the number of troops I can spare to keep Maceo in Pinar del Rio, but you can believe me that they are enough. He will flop like a fish in a basket, doing nothing, until he dies."

151

"Antonio Maceo die?"

"With him confined, the rest will be easy. It will be bloody! I can't deny that. The state of rebellion is such that there must be blood, great outpourings of it. I don't glory in this, but neither do I regret it. Many men must be killed."

"And women and children?"

"That, too, we cannot help. My reconcentration orders have been criticized by your countrymen, *señor*."

"Well, somewhat."

"Somewhat? Furiously!"

George shifted a little in his chair. Each time Weyler looked at him he felt a shock of chill. It was as though something clammy had been pressed against him.

"You are not taking notes, *señor?*"

George had thought of a liquor breath, and of arrogance, but he hadn't prepared a few pieces of paper. Grinning, he tapped his temple.

"It's all here, sir."

"I hope so. My relations with the Yankee press have not been . . . well . . . felicitous."

All butter, George grinned again.

"I should hate to think, sir, that my own little part in the feeling between our nations would not be . . . well . . . felicitous too."

"Um. I hope so. They call me the Butcher. You've heard that?"

"Who hasn't?"

"And I don't love it. I don't glory in it. I shudder at it, as any decent man might. But then, don't you esteem me a decent man, *señor?*"

Jogged, George sat up straighter.

"Sir, you are the governor-general of Cuba."

"That much at least is undisputed."

Minutes were flicking past. There was no clock here.

"Would I be true to my oath if I vacillated the way Campos did? Cuba is a part of Spain, *señor.* There is no other way of looking at it. And now, here, *I* am Spain."

152

The black suit, the skimpy sash, were not inspiring. If it hadn't been for those eyes George might have laughed.

"Excellency, I guess you've got hold of an idea there. But to tell the truth, my paper," went on George, who could not remember what paper he was supposed to be representing, "might like something more . . . well . . . *personal.*"

"You have not made yourself clear. And may I remind you that we have scant time left? I am about to take my bath."

"Well, *that,* sir, for one thing."

"What?"

"Your bath."

"What in the world has my bath got to do with the American public?"

"Why, it might have a great deal, sir. You are thought of as inhuman. I hate to use a word like that—"

"I am accustomed to words like that."

My paper thought that maybe if I could get something *intimate* about you, sir—your habits. Not so much your philosophy of war; not so much your tactics in putting down the rebellion—"

"Restoring order."

"Sure, restoring order. They *know* you mean to do that, sir. But if they could learn something about the way you live."

General Weyler regarded him for a long time, while George shivered. Weyler nodded, and abruptly rose. He drew a watch.

George gulped in joy. For he had been lucky. The rumors were true. This man's bath was his pride. He delighted in an opportunity to display it. He was human, after all—at least in this one respect.

"It four minutes before four, Señor MacPhail. But no doubt in those four minutes you can learn what you seek about my bathroom."

"Why, sure. If you'll just be good enough to show me where it is."

"Come this way, please."

153

CHAPTER XXVIII

HE HEARD it the instant he stepped into the room. This was a huge room, all tiled in light blue, spectacular yet not garish. But George had no eyes for this. He only knew the ticking .

He couldn't localize it: it seemed to come from all parts of the room at once. It was loud; and George believed that his ears must be twitching to it, as a man's nose will twitch at an acrid odor.

Neither of the others appeared to hear this crashing sound. Tick . . . tick . . .

An attendant, no more than a boy, was clad in white, his legs bare and his feet in straw scuffs. Probably he was a civilan, since at the entrance of the govenor-general he did even come to attention, much less salute. He was piling towels.

The tub, an oversized one, much too big for the puny personage who soon would step into it, stood two-thirds full of water from which steam lazily rose. There were several kinds of soap, each in its separate dish, and there were dusting powder, *eau de cologne,* and sundry ointments and ungents. Indeed, the chamber was more like that of a courtesan than that of the world's most brutal soldier. And Antonio Maceo—how *he* would have filled that tub! How *he* would have gloried in this room!

Tick . . . tick . . .

Was it George's imagination? Could he be hearing some-

154

thing that was not there, as might a man in a house said to be haunted?

Tick . . .

It was clear, distinct, to *him!* But the others paid no attention.

Was there a clock somewhere in this room, a clock concealed by, say, towels? If the others knew of the existence of such an instrument it would explain their serenity. For they would have heard. They *must* be hearing!

Tick . . . tick . . .

There were rattan chairs, and a blue wooden bench, all heaped with fluffy Turkish towels, white, black, lemon-yellow.

"I am glad you like it, *señor*. I confess I do. Only when I am here can I feel like a gentleman. And now, if you'll forgive me—"

He began to unbutton his shirt.

He must have divined George's admiration from the glint in George's eye, or perhaps he imagined it, or assumed it. For George himself had said nothing, and neither had he moved, or even looked around. He stood perfectly still, listening.

Now! It came from one of the piles of towels, in a far corner!

"I envy you," he managed. "You should be congratulated. Especially on those towels. May I touch them?"

"*Señor*, I must point out that it is the hour of my—"

But George already had crossed the room to the far pile of towels, and he was ostensibly, fingering them; the fact was, he was probing.

He came upon the thing almost immediately. He did not see it, but he could feel it, a metal box perhaps four inches square, nine or ten inches long, perfect for the purpose. It was heavy, as he learned when he slipped it out, meanwhile mouthing ecstatic remarks about the texture of the towels.

Bent far over, he slipped the bomb under his coat on the left side, pushing it behind the suspender belt there. He

155

was buttoning his coat as he turned, still praising the towels. But he had his right hand over one end of the thing he'd extracted, the end from whence the sounds came. With frantically scrabbling fingers he was tearing at its top.

Weyler had his watch out again.

"*Señor,* it is almost seven minutes beyond my bath time."

"Sorry, general. It isn't often a guy gets a chance to see a plant like this."

"Are you all right, Señor MacPhail?"

"All right?"

"You look pale, and you're sweating. Some pain?"

George had worked the end off the bomb, and now his forefinger entered it, slipping past the clockwork.

Tick . . . tick . . .

Were they deaf that they didn't hear?

He succeeded in smiling, though the smile might have been unsettling to see.

"Gas," he explained, jiggling his right elbow. "It gets me at funny times, sir."

He turned away, doubling over as though in pain. Now his fingernail had been wedged under the edge of the detonating cap. He could feel it there. But it slipped. He found the same edge again and worked it back and forth.

When he spoke again it was in an unnaturally loud voice, in order to drown the sound of the ticking.

"Excuse me. I'll be all right in just a second."

He couldn't force the cap out. Desperate, he crooked his finger to feel for and find the clockwork. He got a cog, and pressed it.

The ticking stopped.

George righted himself, and turned back. In his ears the silence rang, but neither of the others appeared to notice it. The boy went about his work, impassive, dapper. Weyler, peevish, was untying his necktie with one hand, while in the other he held an opened watch.

"If I called a physician——"

"Oh, no, sir, I'm all right now! And thank you for letting

156

me see this room."

Weyler did not offer to shake hands. George was glad of this. He would as soon have fondled a snake. He made a brief bow, jerkily.

"Good bye, sir. And long life to you."

"Luis, show him to Colonel Escribano's office."

The walk down the hall seemed endless, George was all the while aware of that gun on his right hip, that box of dynamite directly over his heart. He looked for, but failed to find, a water closet. He was about to ask the boy where one was when they arrived at the secretary's office.

Escribano was overpolite. He all but fawned upon George.

"I trust that your visit was fruitful?"

"Oh, sure. Fruitful."

"To meet General Weyler is always a pleasure."

"Uh-huh. And a privilege too."

Escribano caught at that word, repeating it. Obliquely he surveyed the results of a recent manicure, as he pointed out that a privilege ordinarily should be paid for.

"What's that?"

"Surely, Señor MacPhail, you have not forgotten our agreement?"

"Oh, no. No, of course not."

"We did not put it into writing, for after all we are men of the world, you and I, is it not so?"

"Absolutely."

"But I am sure that my messenger would recall the verbal arrangement. Should I send for him, to refresh your memory?"

"That's not necessary."

"Then if you will—"

There was a knock, a discreet cough, and a clerk entered.

"You will excuse me, señor?"

"Sure."

After some whispering, Escribano turned, a shade impatiently.

"It is regretable, señor, but the commander of the palace guard objects that you were not searched when you entered."

"What of it? Did they think I'd be carrying a bomb or something?

"Of course not. But it's a regulation, and the commander is a conscientious man. They passed you through because it was known that you were already late for an appointment with the governor-general, who doesn't like lateness. But they feel that they must search you now, on the way out."

"Hell, that's just silly! If I'd had a bomb I'd've tossed it right away, wouldn't I? I wouldn't wait until I got outside again!"

Escribano showed real distress. He had selfish reasons, George believed. Through some intermediary he had struck a bargain with Earl Bronson MacPhail for the interview with the governor-general. It would be payable immediately after the event, and Escribano didn't want anything to go wrong. Maybe he needed the cash this very afternoon? Or he could be fearful that George might repudiate the whole deal, exposing him.

"Silly, yes," he said placatingly. "So many regulations are silly. But at the same time . . ."

He had a thought. He opened a drawer, took out a form, skidded this across the desk.

"If you signed this, *señor*, I think I might quiet the commander of the guard. It testifies that you were searched but that every courtesy was extended. There have been complaints of roughness, and the commander covers himself in this way."

"Fair enough." George, standing, read the thing, which was innocuous and short. "Well, I could sign that. Have you got a pen?"

"Here you are, *señor*. Won't you sit down?"

George did sit down and the clockwork under his coat began to go again.

Tick . . . tick . . .

It was like the beating of his heart, and when he thrust a hand under the coat and slipped a finger over the mechanism it was as though he had extinguished his own life, instead of saving it.

158

How many ticks were left? Not many, surely. It was now four-seventeen, seven minutes after the time at which the thing was set to go off, and the clock had been stopped for no more than ten minutes.

He must not let it tick again. The margin was too narrow.

"Are you sick, *señor?*"

Had he not been so taut, concentrating so fiercely upon his predicament, he would have laughed at that question. For the second time in a quarter-hour somebody had asked about his health; he who had a cast-iron stomach! Nevertheless, it was a cover-up, an excuse. He seized upon it. He rose, nodding miserably, his hand still clutching the thing under his coat.

"Yes. Too much excitement. If I could . . . Would you show . . .?"

"Sandoval!"

The clerk, a moon-faced lad with spectacles, moved swiftly. Holding George by an elbow, he propelled him out of the office, down another hall, and through a narrow doorway, thoughtfully closing the door, leaving himself outside.

Now at last George could get a look at the thing he'd been hugging to his bosom like the Spartan boy and his wolf. There was not much light in this narrow high-ceiling room, which had a stone floor. There was no window, only a transom over the door. But at least he could take the thing out and, holding it close to his eyes, squinting, examine it.

No notable degree of cunning had gone into its manufacture. It was simple, a good point. Bomb makers who fooled with sulphuric acid, uptilting vials, contact wires, automatic sparks, calcium phosphide, and all the rest, George knew, not infrequently wound up with duds. Ballete had not done this. Into his tin box, as he had related, he'd thrust two tied-together dynamite sticks, one of them capped. He had filled the free space with nails, which accounted for much of the weight, but had saved room at one end for a plain alarm-clock mechanism. It could hardly fail to go off within a minute or two of the time set, even if kicked around, even if dumped into water.

159

That mechanism was singularly stubborn, dogged. The instant George removed his finger it started to tick again.

But now, able to see, able to hold the thing in both hands, he could get a firmer fingernail underneath the edge of he detonating cap, which he managed to work out.

He all but went limp, he tottered, and his exhalation might have been loud enough for the waiting-outside Sandoval to hear.

All that remained was to get rid of the thing.

This would not be easy: there was no window, no ventilator, nor was there any niche or slit in the walls. If he threw the decapped bomb over the transom, it would fall upon or very near Sandoval. He could not flush it down the toilet. The water chamber, or the reservoir? But that was a rectangular wooden box high up near the ceiling. Even when standing on the seat George couldn't reach into that box. He was a tolerably good hand with a horseshoe. His nerves, despite the strain lately put upon them, were in good shape; yet he hesitated to try to toss into that water chamber. It was very near the ceiling. Also, it might be covered: he couldn't see. A miss would be noisy.

He sighted again, somewhat less fervently, and put the whole thing into his left hip pocket, carefully covering it with his coat. He went out to the hall.

"Is the *señor* feeling better?"

"Much better, thank you."

He wasted no time. Though there was no longer any danger of an explosion, he had not smashed the clockwork, as perhaps he should have done; at any moment the damned think might start ticking again. So George promptly signed the guard's release form.

"I regret that you did not see fit to complete our understanding right here and now, Señor MacPhail," Escribano said feelingly.

"It was stupid of me."

"But I assume that at your hotel . . ."

"Oh, of course! If you could assign me a messenger . . ."

160

"Sandoval, you will go with Señor MacPhail. He will give you two hundred pesos for the Palace Personnel Relief Fund."

"No receipt will be necessary," George said hastily.

He had been jarred by the size of the bribe. He had but little more than that left of the money sent from Jacksonville. It was in his pocket. He could have paid it over immediately, and would have done so if Escribano made any move to summon his original messenger, since that messenger assuredly would have looked at George, crying, "Why, that isn't Señor MacPhail!" However, Sandoval was all right. Perhaps he was accustomed to being sent on such errands. Surely he showed no amazement. And his presence might mean prestige at the gate.

George and Colonel Escribano shook hands, George murmuring that it was a pleasure to be permitted to contribute to the Palace Personnel Relief Fund.

The door, the gate as well, showed no block. George was even saluted.

Two squares away, cursing himself for an absent-minded fool, and explaining that he'd just remembered that he had the money with him after all, he stopped the carriage. He paid a startled Sandoval, and paid the driver, too, begging Sandoval to keep the carriage for the trip back to the palace and to extend to Colonel Escribano his humble regrets for the delay. He said he would prefer to walk back to the Mascotte, for he needed the exercise.

He saw the carriage off; then, with less than twenty pesos left, he went not to the Mascotte but to his own hotel.

There was a policeman in the doorway. There was another policeman, an officer, with gold braid, at the manager's desk.

"But I tell you that Señor Gustav Howard is not here now," George heard the manager cry.

He walked right past.

CHAPTER XXIX

HE STEPPED INTO a doorway, from which he could watch the hotel entrance. This might have been an uncalled-for precaution. The police could have come on a routine visit, something about alien registration, some new law or military regulation. Still it could be something else, too.

It seemed a week, but it was only a few hours ago that he had gone to the post office to pick up a money order mailed to Gustav Howard by the Chinese financier in Jacksonville. He had *thought* that he was unwatched on that occasion. He had little respect for the Havana police, and believed it all but incredible that even if he'd been spotted they could have traced him so soon. Yet, there might be an elite corps in the department, a sort of uniformed detective squad? And it was true that they could have got the name and address of this hotel, a small one, from the Bank of Spain, which had sent a messenger to it.

He prayed that Ana was all right.

A few minutes later he sighed in relief as the cops came out, side by side, to march away. They looked angry.

As soon as they had rounded a corner George went into the hotel. The manager stewed.

"This will bring us a bad name, *señor!* They know there is a woman up there, and that she is not your wife!"

"Shut up. You're in the hotel business, and you've faced this before. Now, did they get in?"

"I wouldn't give them a key unless they had a search warrant. They didn't like it. But as for your friend up there . . . I don't know."

George ran upstairs. He let himself into the room.

Ana had been standing at the windows that opened upon a crazy little balcony over the street. She must have seen the policemen depart. She turned, with a small cry, and went to George. She all but ran.

"You're safe!"

Astounding himself, he kissed her on the mouth hard.

She colored, but continued to look up, very soberly, studying him. After a while she started to lower her head, but changed her mind, and raised her head again, and threw her arms around his neck.

She might have been as amazed as he was. Neither said anything, but they held one another tight.

After a while, as though at a signal given by some third person, they released one another. Darkly blushing, but determined to be practical, for she knew that time was short, Ana went again to the window, turning her back to him.

"I . . . I didn't let them in."

"Good! They didn't see you, then?"

"No. They asked for a Señor Howard."

"That's me."

"But I told them I knew no Señor Howard. And I said they couldn't come in. They rattled the door. They tried a key of some kind, but I had bolted it on the inside here. Then they shouted that they'd break it down."

"And what did you do?"

"I giggled."

"You . . . *giggled?*"

If it had been a device it was a good one. The police had no doubt assumed that they were dealing with a streetwalker, or some other easily picked-up baggage. A giggle would clinch this belief. But the idea that so lovely and so grave a goddess *could* giggle—it was hard to bear, to believe.

"Why not? I can, you know. I don't very often, but I can."

163

He went to one knee and grabbed her nearest hand and began kissing it. He must have looked a fool, but he couldn't help it. Tears scalded his eyes.

With her free hand she fondled his hair.

"You are so chivalrous. The most chivalrous man I ever met."

"I'm no such thing!"

"If you love me it's because I'm so small and helpless."

"I do love you. But I don't think you're helpless."

"But not now, *señor* . . . dear. There isn't time."

He got to his feet, blushing, probably as deeply as a little while ago she had blushed. He examined the box fuse. It was bulky but not heavy, and there was no name or address on it. He'd known this, but he had to do something.

"You go first. It's possible they aren't watching; and, anyway, they don't know what you look like."

"Maybe there's a back door?"

"If there is, then they'd certainly be watching *that*, even if they didn't watch the front. Go ahead. I'll take this, and I'll catch up to you before you get back."

It went off so well that the let-down was heady. George almost feared, as he joined her at the door of Number Seven, that *he* might start to giggle. Even Ballete had removed himself, as Manuelo told them, stamping out in a rage when fourten brought no explosion.

"This," George said, putting down the carton, "must be delivered to a certain point on the Malecón early tomorrow morning. Meanwhile, it might be as well if I stayed off the streets. Could I impose upon you here?"

"I wouldn't have let you go out now anyway," said the Señorita Ana; and he grinned at her.

As it turned out, he was to remain for many days at Seven Calle de la Reina. He often wondered about that house's normal occupants, whom he never saw and so seldom heard; but he wondered even more about the effect of the house upon Ana. She was proper again, even prim. There were no kisses, open or otherwise. There was not even a surreptitious touching of hands or knees. Though hardly a chatterbox, she was ready enough to talk, and she was plainspoken, serious; but there was at all times a touch of propriety in her manner that would suggest a girl who was watched over by a duenna, as indeed Ana ordinarily was. The embrace in that hotel room might never have occurred. It might have been part of a wishful dream. She still called him *señor,* and he called her *señorita.*

The first morning he was up while it yet was dark; and with Manuelo bearing the box of fuse before him, George, his hand on his pistol, only a few steps behind, went to the Malecón. Incredibly, yet inevitably, like the tide, the dour, shriveled old fisherman was there. Passing the fuse to him was a matter of half a minute, without any complication. George said only the single word "Maceo," and the fisherman didn't as much as nod. The reassuring earliness of the hour, and the publicness of the place, averted all suspicion. Scores passed, but nobody paid any attention.

The return to the Calle de la Reina, however, was more ominous. They went by way of the little side street in which George's hotel was located; or at least, Manuelo went that way, to rejoin George a little later with his report. "Despite the hour," Manuelo said, "there was a policeman standing just inside the door." Moreover, as Manuelo passed, this man was being relieved by another, implying a regulated surveillance.

"I guess I'd better not go back," said George.

Thereafter he stayed in the house. For all the presence of his beloved, this was a dull time, day dragging after slow day. There were no books, neither were there any games to play. Not in so many words, but tacitly, George was asked to stay downstairs. He limited himself to the entrance hall, a gloomy pretentious place; the court, not always habitable now that the rains had come again; his own bedroom; and the kitchen. Except for such times as he could talk with the Señorita Ana, the kitchen was his favorite place, for it was cheerier than elsewhere, and multi-odored. Also, though the servants for the most part were silent unsociable persons, there was always the ineffable Manuelo. Striving to kill time, George renewed his Spanish lessons with Manuelo, picking up some rich profanity, and even took lessons in the guitar. The trouble was that Manuelo and Wilma, too, always were a little uneasy when George was in the kitchen. It was not wrong for him to go there—the Señorita Ana herself went there from time to time, to check things—but it was wrong, they seemed to think, for him to *linger* there, to *enjoy* the place.

George's own sleeping chamber was little more than a cell, a closet, opening upon the court. Even if he'd had books he could hardly have spent time there reading: the light was too poor.

George was not without training in the endurance of boredom. There had been many times in the field when for hours on end, for days, there was nothing to do, nothing even to think about, and when a cloud of futility and of utter boredom had pressed down upon him and upon everybody around him like a pall. But in the Sixth Army Corps. a man at least could stretch his legs. The Calle de la Reina was a prison.

"We should go back to the plantation," Ana said once, unexpectedly.

Her use of the word "we," her serene assumption that they whatever the future, would remain together, caused him to sit up.

"Clear across the island? That would be very hard to do."

"Papers could be arranged."

"With enough money anything could be arranged. But the trip! Cuba's torn to pieces. It's been razed and ravished and burned over. The railroads don't run. Horses are hard to get. Spaniards hold the towns, the magazines, the roads. Patriots roam the countryside, but so do the *plateados*."

"With you it would be all right."

"*Señorita*, I'm touched. But one man is only one man. How could I escort you deep into Oriente? And what would

166

you do if you got there? You couldn't rebuild a plantation all by yourself."

"I could try. And with you—"

"*Señorita*, it grieves me to remind you of this, but I am an officer in the Army of the Republic. I can't desert, like a coward."

"There wouldn't be any cowardice about setting up in the ruins of my father's house, so near to Santiago and the *guerrillos* there. But of course if you've taken an oath . . ."

"No, I haven't. I'm not a real officer, I guess. I was just *created* one, on the field, by General Maceo, the way a king used to whip out his sword and create a knight right after battle."

She smiled a little, a rare sight.

"And a knight you are," she murmured. "But couldn't a knight be transferred?"

"Maceo isn't in Oriente. He's in Pinar del Rio."

"I know that," with a touch of asperity. "But Garcia is in Oriente. Maceo could assign you to his staff. Wouldn't that be the same thing?"

"No. I don't feel that I owe allegiance to the Army of the Republic. All *that* ever did was condemn me to death. But with Antonio Maceo it's different; it's personal. Serving under somebody else, even in his name, wouldn't be right."

"Because a middle-aged mulatto—"

"*Señorita*, he's a gentleman!"

"I never said he wasn't." She all but laughed, then squeezed his hand. "Oh, chivalry! chivalry! Out of all the world I would fall in love with Sir Galahad himself!"

"Ana—"

"We'd better get inside. It's going to rain."

At the end of the fourth week, when another five hundred pesos should have arrived for Gustav Howard at the main post office, George fretted. He talked about going for it.

"No," Ana said. "You do not hold a high opinion of our police here in Havana, *señor*, but you should give them credit for persistence. They seek the man who called for that

167

other money order. They may not know he's Colonel Rat-onero, but they do know that Huau sent him money, and they'd take him to La Cabana and ask him why. They ask their questions harshly at La Cabana, *señor*. They use . . . heavy instruments."

"Well . . ."

"You stay here."

"We need money."

"We do," she said equably. "But we need you more."

She had never made a secret of her poverty. Her father's fortune had been in land, crops, and now the plantation brought in nothing, so that she herself, together with Wilma and Manuelo, for months had been living on the Hernandezes.

"And they are not rich, you comprehend, *señor?*"

George himself had no more than half a handful of coins left. But he was not without resources.

"There's that man MacPhail. We could send for him."

"But I have turned him down. You said I should not sit on a platform and let fools fondle me with their eyes!"

"Sure. But he happens to owe me two hundred pesos. I paid for that interview with Weyler, and why can't I pass it on to him. In a little while, as soon as we think it's safe, I'll be slipping out of the city to rejoin my general. When that happens I won't need money. But *you* at least can have the two hundred pesos."

She looked away at his mention of leaving, but she did not break off the talk. She pointed out, instead, that Señor MacPhail might take advantage of such a summons to tip the police. There could be a reward for George. How did they know that there wasn't? They heard nothing, here, from the outside world.

"I won't write him," George said. "You will. You could hint that you might change your mind. He'd come at the double! And then I could confront him. I could make an unholy ass of him if I told the story of how I walked away with his interview. And at the same time I could offer him a chance to buy that scoop at the same price he was prepared to pay for it a little while ago. Why should he go to the police?"

"I don't like to trust a newspaperman."

"Now I'll be firm," said George. "Here, sit down. And start to write.

CHAPTER XXX

STORKLIKE, GAWKY, backed by that dry, naked little bronze boy who upheld the dry bronze fish, Earl Bronson MacPhail knuckled his hips, cocked his horsy head, and squinted at host and hostess, a fury. Yet he was not hostile. He had accepted the situation without any squawk. He had been lured here, and knew it. He no longer hoped to spirit Señorita Pineda to the mainland for a lecture tour. His one thought was to learn how his appointment had been met wtihout him, and by a rank amateur.

"*Why?* I'll believe that you did it, but . . . *why?*"

"Suppose we let that go," said George. "The point is: do you want an account of what he said and what he looked like and all? I mean, do you want to pay two hundred pesos for that?"

MacPhail produced the money with an alacrity that was breathtaking. He produced also pad and pencil. All joints, like a camel that settles for an unloading, he sat on the bench between them.

"Shoot," he said.

"It isn't much, but—"

"Start talking!"

George told everything he could remember, though leaving out, of course, all reference to the bomb. Not only did he repeat Governor-General Weyler's words but he described the entrance to the palace, the corridors, Colonel Escribano's office, Weyler's office, the celebrated blue bathroom, even the w.c.

MacPhail scribbled fiercely, flipping over page after page.

"That isn't much, I'm afraid," George said at last.

"It's a hell of a lot. Enough for three columns, with what I'll do to it. Now look: you say they all thought you were me?"

"I have no reason to think that they still don't, for that matter; not unless you've gone there since, yourself?"

"No. When I woke up, half an hour too late, I went right to the palace, running. I guess I looked soused. They wouldn't even listen to me. Anyway just a little while before somebody had tried to break through, yelling something about a bomb, and they'd shot him full of holes. The place was in a turmoil. So I gave up, and went back to the Mascotte to sleep the rest of it off. And the next morning I learned that Weyler had left town to inspect the Mariel-Majana *trocha,* and would be gone at least two weeks. Amen."

"The man they killed: did you see the body?"

"Glimpsed it, that's all."

"And he was dead?"

"Oh, plenty dead! A sieve!"

"A young man in a blue coat, cavalry mustache?"

"That's the one."

Whatever else he might have been, MacPhail was no crier over spilt milk. He did not try to cajole Ana. He wasted no time teeth-gnashing in jealousy of one who had scooped *him.* Indeed, his admiration for George was loud.

"When this shindig's over with, any time you want to come back to God's country, look me up, Howard. You'd make a good reporter."

He reached for his hat. George, pleased, rose.

"Oh now, see here—"

"And any time you can find that man Colonel Ratonero for me, I'll make you rich."

"Speaking of men, would your friend Pappachristides be in a position to steer me into a first-class penman?"

171

"My friend Pappachristides *is* a first-class penman. That's how he got his start—*and* why he left Europe. I doubt that you'd find a better forger this side of Florida. Why? Thinking of going east, young man?"

"I have a friend who might want to. Not me. In fact, I'm going the other way. A date with another celebrity."

"Oh? Who is it this time?"

"Antonio Maceo."

The effect of this upon Earl Bronson MacPhail was extraordinary. He had been about to depart, the sloppy cynical correspondent, the man who could never be shocked, who knew everybody and had seen everything. Now he stopped short!

"Why . . . why . . . wher've you folks been? Don't you get any papers here? Don't you ever go out?"

"What's the matter? Has anything happened to General Maceo?"

"No, nothing much. Just that he got killed."

It was a blow between the eyes. George shook his head, like a groggy boxer, to clear it. He told himself that Havana lived on rumors, and that there would always be wild stories about so sensational a figure as General Maceo, a bravado who would gallop to the place where the fighting was hottest. Dead? Nonsense! Look at Ballete y Sierra! How often did a man have to be killed before he stayed that way? George shook his head again, refusing to believe.

"No," in a flat voice.

"Details are a little mixed," MacPhail admitted, "but there isn't a doubt that it happened. One night last week, near Punta Brava. Maceo was riding out ahead of his men—"

"Yes. He always was."

"Physician named Zertucha with him. Also Frank Gomez, the son of old Maximo himself. And a few others. I don't have their names. Zertucha was captured. As near as I can make out, the two parties surprised one another in the dark, and began blasting away. Then they both retreated. But the rebels came right back, once they'd missed Maceo and

172

Gomez. And they found 'em. Dead. No doubt of it. Rebel physician himself, not Zertucha, man named Valiente, took the bullet out. And when he said dead he meant it."

"Yes . . . Colonel Valiente."

"The rebels themselves have admitted it. Officially. Miro's suceeded him in command."

George sat down again. He felt cold inside, and he was dizzy. It was as if he had fallen a great distance, so that no blood was left in his head. Sweat formed on his face like chunks of ice. The world rocked.

"Antonio Maceo . . ."

"Funny thing is, the report went out that he'd been traveling under a flag of truce. That simply wasn't so, but the boys at Tampa put it on every wire, and the whole U. S. A.'s madder than it's been since that man Heritage got shot at Purisima Concepcion. Maceo's a hero."

"He always was," George muttered.

"Listen to this. Just came this morning." MacPhail whisked a newspaper from his pocket. "This was introduced into the Senate at Washington by Senator Call of California. I quote: 'Resolved: That the killing of General Antonio Maceo, a renowned officer in service of the Republic of Cuba, if true, while under a flag of truce, and with the assurance of safety from the Spanish governor-general was a violation of the rules of civilized war, an outrage of base treachery, a murder, cowardly and disgraceful, which demands the execration of every government and of all the people of the world.' "

That politician's rhetoric rolled right past George Heritage: they were like a distant surf.

" '. . . that the government which authorizes, permits, or fails to punish the assassins . . . is an outcast from the family of nations, and from the pale of civilization and public law . . .' "

Maceo was dead. George hoped that he'd been hit while his mouth was open on a shout, while his strong teeth showed. George hoped that he had received the perfume

173

and cigars. Antonio Maceo would have suffered without his perfume.

" '. . . and that the Committee on Foreign Relations be directed to make inquiry as to the facts, and report to the Senate at an early date.' Well, it amounts to a recognition of Cuban independence, practically a declaration of war against Spain. They won't pass it, of course. They won't even vote on it. But it shows the way some folks feel."

Automatically the host in a house that wasn't his, George showed this visitor to the door. But George's ears were ringing, and he scarcely heard the farewell. When he returned to the court, he stood for some time in silence, chin low, his feet spread.

When at last he noticed Ana, who had not stirred, he nodded.

"All right. We'll go east. We'll go back to the plantation."

"The passes—"

George took the pistol from his pocket, broke it, and spun the chamber. He closed it, satisfied.

"I'll get the passes," he promised; then he went outside.

CHAPTER XXXI

FROM SAN CRISTOBAL DE LA HABANA to Santa Clara, not much more than 150 miles as the crow flies, was closer to two hundred by rail. This took them five days; and it rained ceaselessly.

A great deal of time, even during daylight hours—at night the train stood still, while soldiers were sentries around it—they were motionless. Even when they moved, it was with a series of hesitant, uncertain jerks. No explanation was vouchsafed for these halts. Some might have been due to mechanical trouble, for the engine wheezed and groaned. Many, surely, were because of the need to examine the track ahead for possible explosives. Short of every gully and bridge, howsoever small, the train was stopped, and a couple of soldiers would unlimber a handcar from the tender and pump this a certain distance ahead and then back, very slowly.

"There are times," Ana told George, speaking low and in English, "when I wish that you had never even seen a mousetrap."

Many of the stops, too, were military. The railway line was stippled with fortlets, blockhouses, watch towers, and each of these had to be supplied or its garrison relieved. The full-night stops were always made in the shadow of an army post.

In addition to the engine, the tender, and a sort of command caboose in the rear, the train consisted of two cars filled with freight, most of it food; a car for soldiers; and a car for paying passengers, of whom the four from the Calle de la Reina were the only ones who made the full trip; the others being, to them, shifting, faceless, without color.

Wilma, an Indian, and Manuelo, indefatigibly the peasant, settled themselves stolidly side by side. It was as though each had pulled a shade over the window of his soul. Their eyes were veiled, and they did not speak. When they were yanked or bumped by the movements of the train, they rocked in their seats like straw dummies.

For the Señorita Ana it was harder; and it was hardest of all for George Heritage.

He was worried. It had taken five days for him to locate Nikos Pappachristides and to coax and bully out of that Greek, at the moderate price of ten pesos each, four separate *cedulas,* or army passes. They had spent somewhat more than this making up their basket. "Don't they have a diner on this train?" George had grumbled. Moreover, their tickets, like their passes, were not good beyond Santa Clara. Indeed the railroad went no farther.

Where they would live there, how they would pay for food in a city sure to be crammed with peasant-prisoners, the *reconcentrados,* and how they would get away in an easterly direction; these were matters left in the lap of fortune. The Señorita Ana was placid. There were friends of her father at Santa Clara, she said.

"If they're still alive," muttered George.

The windows had been boarded against possible ambush, so that the car was dark. To look out it was necessary to peer through a crack like a boy at a ball game. There was little enough to see anyway; and this was not because of the rains, which in fact at times attained a certain terrible grandeur. Cuba was a land that was dead.

Ana told George that ordinarily the soil of the fields in such a province as this, a lush one, would be of three colors: black for sugar, red for coffee, light brown for tobacco. What

176

they saw most during those five dreary days were fields of a sickly, dirty, dark brown—cane fields that had been burned. Now and then there would be the skeleton of a wrecked mill, or the charred timbers of a plantation house. In most cases, the jungle, with eager-reaching fingers, was taking these over, enveloping them. Almost never was there in sight one of those thatched huts, *bohoios*, that, like the royal palms, would have played so prominent a part in any pre-war Cuban landscape. Why anybody should take the trouble it was hard to see, but these too had been burned. They were represented, generally, by round, black piles of ashes. "Ink spots," George and Ana called them. Often they stretched as far as the eye could see.

No men moved in this wilderness. No smoke stood wavering against the sky. No birds flew, excepting, here and there, the clumsy low-wheeling buzzard.

Somehow, at last, they made it. They spent half an afternoon shivering in a leaky station while Manuelo scoured the town for the friends of the late Don Diego Pineda. These proved to be Negro, which amused George.

"The Underground Railroad in reverse, eh?"

"A tunnel? I do not understand?"

It took a long while to explain it to her; but then, they had plenty of time.

"Yes. There was slavery here too, until a few years ago."

"There still is," said George, who had glimpsed the *reconcentrados*.

Unlike the Hernandez family, the Selvas were immediately and most solicitously concerned with the welfare of their guests. They had little enough, but what they did have was pressed upon George and Ana. Disregarding the rain, Manuelo and his wife searched the town for food and information; but the Señorita Ana always was guarded by her hostess, a plump intense Negress. Ana went out-of-doors occasionally for exercise, but it depressed her to see the thousands of peasants who had been stripped from their countryside and driven into the town like cattle. There they slept in alleys or in the most ragged of tents on the outskirts, many of them sick, all of them hungry, bewildered. George, however, was kept indoors, and he was cautioned to stay away from windows. Most of the time he spent in the cellar, where he slept. He would talk with Ana or practice the guitar and learn Cuban folk songs from Ana, whose treble was small, though her memory was large, and from Madame Selva, who had a robust contralto.

He spent nine days in this fashion, and they were comfortable days, even gay. He was to look back at them with a wistful sigh many times during the miserable months that followed.

The Selvas had urged them to wait in hiding, until the end of the rains. This they had refused to do, for two reasons. One reason was their eagerness to get back to the Pineda plantation and learn its, and their fate. The other reason was that George thought that, when the rains had ceased, otherwise lazy bandits might roam the land; and it was these he most feared, the *plateados,* the utterly unabashed lawless, who would kill for a peseta, and who saw only one reason to take a female prisoner.

"There are no pickings left for them," Dr. Selva had cried. "You have not been out here in more than a year, señor, and you do not know what it's like. I tell you, it's Sahara."

"I took a look now and then, on the way here," George had replied. "Sometimes I saw a buzzard. Where there are buzzards there will be *plateados,* the next lowest thing."

The Selvas at least had insisted upon giving them food, clothing, hammocks and a machete, the collection of which took much time. But without these supplies, as they soon learned, they could never have hoped to get into Oriente Province.

As Dr. Selva had said, the land was a desert. They had thought to avoid towns, even villages, and never to travel on any road; but there were no villages or towns, only black ruins, and the roads, ankle-deep in mud, were deserted, like everything else.

178

Twice they did encounter small parties of horsemen who might have been bandits. These men, who seemed somewhat unsure of themselves, asked a few questions—questions George flatly refused to answer. Though they did eye the *señorita* thirstily, it was clear that they were after easier game. George faced them each time with his hand on the butt of his revolver, which he was wearing openly now. After a while they growled something and rode away, with George watching them until they were out of sight.

There was another occasion when a large group of what were surely *guerrillos* encamped on the edge of a wood, in the center of which the party from the Calle de la Reina had made their own camp. What these men were doing in that remote bleak place, the homeless ones were never to learn. Though they cast about a bit for firewood, they seldom penetrated deeply into the wood, being more interested in the plain. Perhaps they had planned to waylay some person, or some party, on the nearby road? Whatever the reason, they stayed there for four days, during which time the fugitives existed on cold food, being afraid to light a fire, and huddled piteously in their hamocks. It rained all the while.

They got so that they scarcely spoke to one another! even the gregarious Manuelo was silent. While the mud was there, every step was agony. Finding food was the most difficult thing of all. Seemingly the land had been seared; even Manuelo and Ana had trouble finding fruits; but the stout Wilma, apparently from nowhere, again and again produced tamarinds, pomegranates, oranges, figs, grapes. Twice she found green coconuts, rather rancid to the taste, but they ate these. Often she unearthed roots the very appearance of which caused a stomach to go queasy; but they ate these, too, raw. Once they came upon a cabbage palm, miraculously whole, and this they cut down for its center, which, when chopped up, much resembled cole slaw. All the gullies, of course, were flooded, all the streams were high; but they never did catch a fish: fishing took up too long. However,

179

Manuelo did turn out to be an expert machete thrower, and three times he got rabbits, which were plentiful; once, he brought down a *jutia,* a small tree bear. The rabbits were delicious. The *jutia* was not; it was rank, but they ate it just the same.

Without spoken agreement they abstained alike from complaints and from false cheeriness. Wilma, as always, scarcely opened her mouth, though she could do a great deal with a grunt. Manuelo, who might have been getting on to middle age, took the whole thing hard; clearly he suffered the most, though he suffered in silence. The one who suffered the least, or at any rate showed it the least, was, unexpectedly, the Señorita Ana. She kept, somehow, that aspect of doll-like fragility, but in truth she was as tough as a nut. She never whimpered, even involuntarily.

When at last the rains did cease, suddenly, like a bath shower that's been shut off, and the sun came out again, they glowed in relief as their clothes steamed; but they gave forth no whoops of joy. The sun, too, could be harsh, they knew, but undeniably it was better to be dry. And soon they would be able to sleep on the ground.

Now at last they did make it a point to avoid travel on the roads, such as those were. Instead, they paralleled them, watching both ways.

Three nights later, the ground once more was dry, and it was with a sense of luxury that they spread their hammocks upon it, spreading the blankets over the hammocks. Hung from trees, the hammocks always had been lumpy. They had but two of them: Ana and Wilma sleeping in one, George sleeping with Manuelo, who snored but at least was not full of lice. Manuelo never did express a longing to be with his wife. His was the resignation of his race; and he took it for granted that Wilma's nursely duties to the *señorita* were of more importance than the demands of their marriage.

Customarily, the two couples slept some distance apart, for the sake of decency. This night, George went up to the women's bed, which was on slightly higher ground; in part to see if he could do anything for them, fetch them anything, in part to take a last look around the countryside before the sun set.

Ana was staring at him very strangely. Wilma was looking at Ana.

They had eaten well, a hot meal and, since there were not many mosquitoes in this high place—and since the night was mild—they should sleep well too. George said as much.

Ana kept looking at him.

George studied the stars, just tumbling into their places in a cobalt sky. He had never been much of a hand for stars, but like a man at sea in a rowboat he had learned that the position of Orion or of Cassiopeia's Chair can mean a great deal when your life happens to be at stake. Among the gifts from the kindly Selvas there was no compass.

"We may be working a little too far south, too near the mountains," he murmured. "Remind me to check the courses of the streams tomorrow."

Ana said suddenly to her maid, "Go down to Manuelo."

Wilma started to weep. She sobbed loudly, shattering the silence of dusk. It was as though an alligator had burst into song. It was shocking, throat-catching, if not quite real.

"Go down to him!"

The thick Indian, fully dressed, clumped out of the bed. Her shoulders were heaving, her face glistered with tears. She did not glance at George, but with a heavy step made her way toward Manuelo, weeping all the while.

The last rinsings of a chill, lemon-colored sunset were washed away. The stars, tentative till now, openly took over the sky.

Ana Pineda threw aside the blanket. She was wearing only a short linen slip, her legs and arms bare.

"Come," she said. "It has been too long."

CHAPTER XXXII

MOST DESOLATE of all, more desolate than the land over
which they had approached it, was the Pineda plantation.
In the shadow of the Sierra Maestra range, it looked as
though a peak had toppled upon it: it resembled some great
squashed lizard, back broken, eyes no longer beady, scales
no longer bright.

Obviously it had been visited since George and Captain
Ballete came upon the lacerated body of Don Diego. No
doubt the *guerrilleros* had returned to finish the job. There
was not much more that they could have done outside. The
mill machinery was too heavy to be dragged away, but it
had been smashed with sledge hammers, and the building
itself burned, like the stables, like the living quarters of the
seasonal field hands. The pigs and chickens and geese and
milch cows had been driven away, together with the riding
and carriage horses. Not so much as a mongrel dog, a
mangy cat, skulked about the premises. The cane fields had
been burned, the cacao grove hacked to shreds, and every
fruit tree in the orchards chopped down. Even the modest
family vegetable garden had been spaded up. The cooking
kiosk, a wooden structure, had been burned to the ground.
The house itself, being made of stone, had resisted the
torch; but whatever could be done to deface it had been
done. Doors had been torn off their hinges. There never
had been any glass at the windows, but the jalousies and storm

shutters had been smashed with an ax. The pieces had been heaped in the center of each room, and burned, the lime-washed ceiling thereby being blackened. Into those bonfires had been tossed the torn or splintered bits of such napery, tapestry, and furniture as the vandals scorned to carry off.

No doubt because it was unmarked, and they couldn't find it, the grave of Don Diego had not been desecrated. George took Ana there, and she knelt, with George turning his back to her.

It was well to look far away, since everything near at hand was depressing. He studied the hills. Until this time they had been untapped. A mining engineer ought to be called in to examine them for possible underground wealth. At the worst, they were well wooded, mostly with pine. A sawmill could be packed up, when peace came, and there would soon be planks and beams enough to rebuild the mill. Dynamite would blast out the stumps. And then pineapples could be planted.

"Yes, what we need is pineapples," he said aloud, though he was speaking only to himself.

"What we need," said Ana, speaking not all to herself, "is a priest."

"Oh, I'm sorry, dear!'

He hastened to help her rise. She frowned a mite, for she did not like to be helped.

He said, "A priest, yes. But maybe a physician too? Don't you think we might send Manuelo for a physician?"

"Oh, I'm all right. It won't be for months yet, and Wilma can take care of me. The *guerilleros* might follow a physician, but even those devils wouldn't trail a priest."

"That's true."

"Anyway, we don't want the baby to be born out of wedlock."

"Certainly not," he shouted, shocked that she should even put words to such a possibility.

If they had been able to devise any schedule for their trek through Cuba, they would have been, at this time at

183

their destination, two months late. The reason for this was Wilma, who, shaken by the loss of her duennaship—the fall, as she saw it, of her beloved Señorita Ana, her mistress—had done something George would not have supposed her capable of: she had fallen ill. It was a fever, but not yellowjack, which at its worst would have been over, one way or the other, within a couple of weeks; nor was it malaria, for there were no chills, only a high temperature that continued night and day. The woman made no whimper. Though her eyes were open most of the time, it was not always certain whether she was conscious. She never answered any question. She lay on her back and stared at the ceiling; that was all.

They had carried her into a hut. This was in a tiny village, a mere hamlet, which for some reason not evident had been spared by both sides, a somnolent spot. Still, it was the sort of place these travelers might ordinarily have avoided. With Wilma ill, they caught up their breath and marched in. They rented a rickety mud-and-thatch hut furnished with a charcoal brazier and two flimsy cots, and there they stayed for two months, nursing her, at the same time staving off questions. This was easy enough for George, who pretended to know no Spanish, but Ana and Manuelo, already anxious for their patient found it trying.

They felt safe, if not comfortable. There was no military post nearby, and they themselves were so tattered that they could hardly have looked like prizes, to be informed upon in the hope of a reward. In all truth, they *were* poor, having hardly one *real* to rub against another. They had been obliged to haggle about the price of the hut; even finding food that they could afford had been hard.

Ana and Manuelo, the one quiet, tireless, efficient, the other emotional, tearful, but faithful too, had been the nurses. It was delicately put to George that perhaps Wilma did not wish to see him, so he kept out of the hut as much as possible. Yet sometimes he would sit on the other cot, watching Wilma in profile, marveling at that craggy, adamant personality.

Though the fever was genuine, there were times when George wondered whether the old woman was not deliberately *willing* herself to die, *forcing* her ailment. There was no crisis, and when she began to get well she did so very slowly. She could hardly have been faking that. Indeed, when she rose, it was at her own insistence, and she started on the long walk again much earlier that she should have done.

Yet they had made it, somehow.

There was so much to do, so much to clean up, and they were so tired, that several days passed before Ana and George conferred on their future course.

George would have favored going to Santiago-de-Cuba, where he could throw himself upon the mercy of the U. S. Consul, except that such a course would mean leaving Ana with no more protection than the two servants. If Ana went with him she might be recognized. The estate could have been expropriated—it probably had been—and Ana might be arrested on a simple change of trespassing on her own property!

"We could be married first; then, as my wife, you'd be an American citizen, and the Consul would have to take care of you too."

"But that wouldn't include Wilma and Manuelo?"

"No."

"Then we'll stay here. We'll send for the priest to come to us."

This was easier to say than to do. The best of the four to go was Wilma. Ana was too well-known both in Purisima and Santiago; so too was Manuelo, who, before he settled into marital life, had gone about a bit, had been, truly, something of a blade. George as a foreigner would be suspect; also he would not know how to approach a priest. While the country folk might be assumed to be rebels, as might most of those in the towns, so far as the persons at the Pineda plantation knew there were still soldiers and guerrilleros alike at both Santiago and Purisima. A recognized messenger might inspire some of the men who'd been here to come again. And there was no defence. There was only George and his revolver, Manuelo and his machete.

"I wish we knew a little more about what might be happening in the world," George grumbled.

"Why should we, *señor?*" Manuelo asked.

"Well, it might help. It's been months since we heard anything."

Wilma, elected, was coached in her part, a part she was more than willing to play, since the attachment of her mistress to a *Yanqui* weighed upon her soul, and she, the discarded duenna, strove to correct it.

Thus trained, Wilma set forth. She was not to speak to anybody. She was not to price anything. She was to go directly to the priest at Purisima Concepcion and state her case. She could not pretend that this was an emergency; that would be lying—and she shouldn't lie to a man of God—but she should emphasize the need of the churchly office, if necessary even mentioning the Señorita Ana's condition. In Santiago there would be less chance that somebody might recognize her, but there were many priests in Santiago, any one of whom, appealed to, might ask why the priest at Purisima, so much nearer, wasn't summoned.

They watched her off, grumpy, undeviating. They waved to her, but she never turned her head.

Three days later she was back, saying only that she had seen the priest and that he would come. She had spoken to nobody else. She was sure that she had not been followed.

They were all working, though it was hard to say why. Perhaps their sense of neatness prompted it. They had no neighbors, as they had no resources. Yet neither did they have any other place to go; and nobody likes to live in a shambles. They spent much time gathering food in the foothills, but much, too, in sweeping, scrubbing.

The fourth morning after Wilma had returned, the priest arrived. He was dusty and small, an old man, tired, on an ass. He blessed Ana and George absent-mindedly, accepted a drink of *guarapo* from the one jug that had been left, wiped his mouth with the back of his hand, cleared his throat, and then looked intently at both of them.

For a long while he didn't say anything. George fidgeted. Ana, seated, was circumspect. The servants had not even ventured to enter the room.

"Señorita Pineda and I wish to be married," George said.

"I see."

Naturally he saw that she was pregnant! Why did he have to stall? Was he bullying her? Was he waxing sanctimonious? George began to fluster, unsure of himself.

"May I speak to you first, my son?"

"Why not?"

Without a word, head averted, hands folded before her, Ana left the room. George waited, bristling.

The priest took his time. He had come a long way, and he was in no hurry. Moreover, he was not sure how to approach this angry young man who was not of his own nationality, and not—as the priest seemed to divine—even of his own faith.

"My son," he said at last, "for what you are about to do, forgiveness may be needed. I do not know. But you know. If that is so, do you wish me to ask for the intervention of some saint?"

"I can do my own praying, thanks."

It was a churlish answer, and one for which George was instantly sorry; but the priest, accustomed to insult, ignored it.

"In other words, you don't wish to confess to me?"

"In other words, I'm not willing to admit that I have anything *to* confess."

The priest gave a small smile.

"We all have that, my son. But no matter, now."

George was about to ask what damn business it was of his, anyway; but he curbed this angry question; for after all, it *was* the priest's business.

"Then there are only two things I'd ask you: first, when you propose to be wed to Ana Pinead are you sure that there is no greed for riches in your heart?"

"Riches—?"

George was flabbergasted.

"These are wide lands. I happen to know that they're clear of debt. It would be easy, once a blessed state of peace was restored, to raise money on them, for their rebuilding, replanting. Ana Pineda's brother is dead, her father is dead. Her husband would control her fortune. Had you pondered this?"

"Father, I swear I never even thought of it!"

The priest looked at him, nodding slowly. There was no notable kindness about this old man, nor was he sympathetic; rather, he tended to sarcastic; but he was not a fool.

"I believe you. Now, one more question. You two were thrown together in the wilderness, there nobody could join you in marriage. Nevertheless, what you did was a mortal sin, you know that, don't you?"

"I suppose so."

"Well, I tell you it was. You expiate it by marriage. Is this your one reason? Are you thinking only of the peace of your own soul?"

"I begin to see what you mean. And the answer is 'no,' like to the other one. I give you my word, Father, I would marry Ana if she didn't have an acre and I'd never laid a hand on her."

"Very well. You may go outside. And please ask Ana Pineda to come in with me. She and I are old friends, and we'll have much to talk about."

CHAPTER XXXIII

GEORGE WENT OUT to the head of the lane, the same lane in which he had first kissed Ana.

It was a morning that sang. The sunlight was golden, the air warm and clean.

For the first time since he had returned to it, the Casa Pineda seemed to George alive, even vibrant. It was no longer a ruin. No longer did it have the silence of the grave.

In part, this might have been because of the cleaning-up work they'd already done, or it could have been the weather. George's happiness, too, supposedly had something to do with it; for he was about to marry the woman he loved, and—he who had always been homeless—he was acquiring a home.

Yet there was more. The plantation *sounded* alive. What was that? No field hands chanted, nor did vanes or wagons creak, and there wasn't any birdsong. It was the *bees!* There! The bees hummed tirelessly.

They must raise bees, George decided. He had helped to tend bees in Androscoggin County, and he knew them as the most accommodating of insects. They might swarm now and then, requiring to be coaxed back, but for the most part they'd remain in the hive and keep it immaculate. There was no need to water or feed them. Supply them with ready-made square of comb and they would go to work filling these. You simply took the honey away. You moved, of course, carefully; but as long as you didn't jog them, the bees never resented your presence. So you left them clean wax, and they filled *that* as well. They never appeared to resent the theft. All they asked was flowers.

Yes, decidedly, he and Ana must raise, among other things, bees.

Flowers . . .

Where would they find flowers here? There were butterflies tumbling across the lane too, he noticed. Yet the *guerrilleros* on their latest visit had taken the trouble to uproot all the bushes in the rose garden, and even to chop down that splendid purple bouganvillea that covered the grating over the terrace. There was no meadow nearby, and surely there were no wild flowers among the charred stumps of sugar cane.

Yet there were butterflies. And bees.

The hibiscus hedge! Because it extended straight before him, along one side of the lane between the doorway in which he stood and the Purisima highway, on the other side of which there was a small wood, he had not noticed it; he had taken it for granted. The hedge, dark green of leaf, was shoulder-high, and was studded with bright red flowers. Why, when they were cutting down everything else, hadn't the *guerrilleros* cut this? It had no thorns, was not tough, would offer little resistance.

Could the hedge have been left standing because it made a cover behind which to approach the house? A man might slip behind it from the wood, with scarcely one chance in a hundred of being seen from the house; then, crouching, make his way to the house itself, surprising it. Without that hedge, even a rush would not do the trick, for men could be picked off from any of the windows.

Did the *guerrilleros* plan to check now and then on the Pineda plantation house? Had they considered the chance that somebody might return?

And had the priest been followed?

George thought he saw something move down there, about halfway to the road.

From bliss so keen that it stung, he went into a state of rage. There was Cuba for you! First a scene of ineffable peace, with sunshine, butterflies, flowers; and then a murderous fury. At one moment a smile, at the next a knife between the shoulder blades.

Now, indisputably, the hedge did stir. Something twinkled there. The muzzle of a rifle showed above topmost leaves.

George spun on his heel and raced back through the house. His pistol, he knew, was in the kitchen.

Ana was on her knees, the priest standing before her.

"Keep away from the windows!"

Back in the doorway, he raised the revolver, cocking it. He stood sideways to the lane, the hedge, so as to present as narrow a target as possible, in the classic position of the duelist. He shouldn't have stood there at all, and he knew this; but his rage was so hot that he could not have remained in hiding.

"Come out with your hands up! God damn it, come out or I'll fill you full of lead!"

In his excitement he used English. But surely his intent was plain, for he obviously meant it. He would have started to shoot.

The response was prompt. Four hands appeared, palms turned toward him, and then two floppy-hatted heads.

"Brother"—it was pure Georgian, U. S. A. "iffen you ain't a Yank, with that voice, then I ain't never heerd one."

"Don't shoot," the other said mildly. "We're U. S. A. Sixteeth Infantry, regular. We wasn't fixin' to hurt nobody. We just plumb got lost."

"We was foraging, an' I reckon we took a wrong turn. Please put that gun down, mister. It makes me nervous."

"United States Army!"

"Well, hell, Mister, do we look like Frenchman or something?"

"How many of you are there?"

191

"Ain't never counted. Fifty thousand, maybe. But they's only us two here, and we'd sure appreciate a drink, Mister."

George turned back in the doorway. The priest stood there, quizzically smiling.

"Father, you never told me the U. S. had declared war on Spain!"

"You never asked."

"How long have they been here?"

"Day before yesterday they landed at Siboney and they're moving on Santiago. It should be all over soon."

"A week's about what we reckon," the Georgian drawled. "Give or take a day or two."

"Mister, how 'bout that drink?" the other one said.

George holstered his pistol. He stepped aside.

"Come in. We've still got some *guarapo,* if you're willing to act as witnesses to a wedding."

"Brother, for a drink, I'd witness any wedding in the world exceptin' maybe my own."

So they arranged themselves, standing, for there were no chairs—in the largest of the rooms, one that had lately been scrubbed, so that ceiling and floor were clear of soot, and the air smelled sweet. The soldiers tugged down their blue tunics, brushed the dust from their puttees and took off their hats. The Georgian even slipped the plug of tobacco out of his mouth and held this behind his back. Manuelo and Wilma, holding hands, beamed from the background. George had unstrapped his pistol. Ana Pineda, though literally in rags, was as trim and clean and as lovely as a cameo. She looked proudly up at George. The priest opened a book.

"George, wilt thou take Ana, here present, for thy lawful wife?"